SNIFFERS AGENCY – THE NOSE KNOWS

A Cozy Mystery

D.M. LITTLEFIELD

&

S.L. MENEAR

BLACK STALLION PUBLISHING

SNIFFERS AGENCY -THE NOSE KNOWS
Copyright © May 2020 by S.L. Menear & D.M. Littlefield
TRADE PAPERBACK & DIGITAL EDITIONS

Black Stallion Publishing
1281 N. Ocean Drive, Suite 149
Singer Island, FL 33404

ISBN-13: 978-1-943264-14-8 PRINT
ISBN-13: 978-1-943264-15-5 EBOOK
10 9 8 7 6 5 4 3 2 1
Cover Design by Patti Roberts of Paradox Book Covers
Cover Picture Created by Artist Michael Castro

Black Stallion Publishing

Dedicated to our family's beloved Blue Jay, Chipper

And to Dottie's dear doggies, Cookie and Lady

And to Sharon's treasured Timber-shepherds,

Pratt and Whitney

And to Quill, an extraordinary African grey parrot

ACKNOWLEDGMENTS

First and foremost, we'd like to thank our Lord and Savior, Jesus Christ, for his many blessings.

We are especially grateful to Niko Bujaj, owner of The Islander Grill and Tiki Bar inside the Palm Beach Shores Resort and Vacation Villas on Singer Island at 181 S. Ocean Avenue, Palm Beach Shores, Florida 33404, phone (561) 842-8282.

Early during the COVID-19 pandemic, Niko called and checked on all his friends and customers, including us. He asked if we needed anything. We explained we were in the high-risk category and that we were unable to find a place to buy toilet paper, hand sanitizer, face masks, and gloves. Niko responded by dropping off a box that contained 28 rolls of toilet paper, a huge container of hand sanitizer, 50 masks, and 100 gloves. He refused to let us pay him. He did the same thing for our neighbor and for many others.

Niko is truly a prince of a man whose kindness and generosity are second to none. If you enjoy delicious food at reasonable prices in a beautiful oceanfront resort, please reward this wonderful man by dining and drinking at The Islander Grill and Tiki Bar, his excellent restaurant and bar. Thank you, Niko!

We'd like to thank Michael Castro, the talented artist who drew the dogs and parrot for our book cover. Michael can draw anything, and he drew the animals exactly as we had imagined them. Thank you, Michael, for bringing our animal characters to life in your amazing art. Michael can be reached via email at artbymikec@gmail.com and his web site is at https://www.mikecastroart.com

ONE

Garnet, Florida

Darcy McKay squinted in the bright sunlight as she drove her white SUV to the Garnet Market and parked. Like all the other buildings in the lakeside town, the grocery store adhered to the town's architectural design code which mimicked a New England village, the only differences being concrete-block construction to withstand hurricanes and pastel colors with white trim. The buildings varied in size from one to three stories.

As she exited her car, a brisk wind caught her long red hair and blew it into her lovely face. Loud cursing drew her attention to a burly man yanking on a miniature dachshund's leash. The little dog struggled to keep pace with its enormous owner, and the brute kicked it. Pain-induced yelps from the dog filled Darcy with rage.

She rushed toward the man, shouting, "Stop hurting that dog!"

When she got closer, she noticed the man's eyes were bloodshot, and his breath reeked of alcohol.

He shouted, "Back off or I'll kick your bossy butt!"

Darcy stood her ground. "You broke the law when you hurt that dog. I could have you arrested."

Bert and Betty Hancock, elderly charter members of the Humane Society, witnessed everything from where they stood outside the Pampered Pup dog grooming shop a little farther down the block.

The drunk glowered at Darcy, who stood only five feet two inches. He launched a kick at her. She nimbly dodged his foot and landed a solid kick to his groin with her pointed leather boot. As he crumpled to the ground, she spotted a tall, muscular man sprinting toward her from across the street.

Good, he's coming to help me.

She glared down at the guy moaning on the sidewalk. "I'm taking your dog to the animal hospital and getting it checked."

He grunted. "Daisy doesn't need help—I do. Call an ambulance."

"Forget it." She knelt down with her back to him and held out her hand, coaxing the trembling dog. It had retreated behind a small shrub. The little dog crawled to her, and she gently cuddled it in her arms and murmured, "Don't worry, Daisy, I won't let him hurt you again."

"I . . . I'll have you arrested for assault," he said, moaning.

"You tried to kick me, and I defended myself."

The dark-haired man who'd crossed the street helped the bully to his feet and flashed his badge. "I'm Detective Scott Logan. You're both coming with me to the police station to settle this."

The dog abuser pointed at Darcy. "I want to press charges against that hellcat. She kicked me."

Darcy glared. "It was self-defense. You'll get my statement later. This little dog probably needs medical attention."

"Miss, if you don't come with me right now, I'll arrest you."

Her green eyes widened. "I don't *believe* this. You can't be serious."

His brows arched over brilliant blue eyes as he looked

down at her. "I'm very serious."

Bert and Betty were still standing in front of the Pampered Pup.

Darcy waved at them and shouted, "You saw what happened. Will you please come to the police station?"

Burt nodded and waved with his right hand. His trembling Yorkie was snuggled under his left arm.

Detective Logan helped the moaning man into the rear seat of his police car as Darcy carried the dog toward her Chevy Suburban.

"Hey, Miss, you need to ride with me to the station." He held the front passenger door open for her.

She scowled. "I was going to follow you. You're making a big mistake." Her face flushed, and her body tensed as she slid into the front seat. Cradling the trembling dog in her lap, she yanked the seat belt down and buckled it.

He slid into the driver's seat. "I don't make mistakes. I do everything by the book."

Annoyed, she stared straight ahead.

Detective Logan parked in front of the police station and helped the limping man up the steps. Darcy walked behind them, gently holding the frightened dog in her arms.

"Hi, Darcy, what's up?" Officer Murphy asked.

She grumbled, "Big trouble. Is the chief in?"

"I'll let him know you're here."

The men on duty gathered around as tall, broad-shouldered Police Chief Joseph McKay walked in.

He asked, "Logan, got any new leads on the arsonist case you're working?"

"Um, I've got an idea I'd like to try." Logan glanced at Darcy and the drunk.

The chief smiled at her and looked at Logan. "I see you've met my daughter. Has she agreed to help you?"

Logan paused, raising his eyebrows. "*She's* your daughter?"

Chief McKay frowned. "Is there a problem?"

The drunk blurted, "Yeah, there's a big problem. She kicked me. I demand you arrest her."

The chief thrust his hands on his hips. "Darcy, what's going on here?"

Her green eyes blazed as she explained what happened and then said, "He wants *me* arrested? I want *him* arrested." She crossed her arms. "I have witnesses who'll corroborate my story."

Bert and Betty Hancock hurried into the room.

"Sorry we're late. I had a difficult time finding a

parking spot," Burt said.

Betty pointed at the dog abuser. "That horrible man should be behind bars where he can't hurt anyone else. He kicked that poor little dog *and* Darcy."

"We both saw him do it," Bert said.

The chief said, "Get the witnesses to sign statements and charge this loser with drunk and disorderly, assault, and animal cruelty."

One of the officers watching the drama took charge.

Officer Murphy grabbed a five-dollar bill slipped into his hand by the dejected looking officer standing beside him. Murphy shoved the bill in his pocket and whispered, "I told you Darcy was in the right. She always fights for the underdog, and I do mean dog."

Darcy overheard him and smiled. She held up the dog. "Dad, I'm taking this dachshund to the animal hospital." She glared at Detective Logan and handed him her business card. "If you still want to talk business with me, call for an appointment, Mr. By-the-Book Hotshot Detective." She turned and hurried out of the building.

Bert and Betty followed her.

TWO

Detective Scott Logan held Darcy's card in his hand, his face crimson.

Chief McKay put his hand on Scott's shoulder. "Let's go into my office."

"I'm sorry, Chief, I didn't know she was your daughter."

"Our job is to enforce the law. It wouldn't have mattered that she was my daughter if she'd committed a crime. *I* would have arrested her. You were just following procedure. No reason to apologize."

"Yes, but did you see the way she glared at me? I don't think she'll ever want to work with me."

"Darcy is quick tempered—comes with being a natural

redhead, but she'll get over it. Let her simmer down before you call for an appointment." Chief McKay ran his hand through his light brown hair and looked up at the ceiling. "On second thought, come to my house for dinner Friday night."

"Are you sure she won't shoot me on sight?"

He grinned. "Well, she *is* an expert shot—taught her myself."

Scott rubbed the back of his neck. "That's not making me feel better. Tell me more about her."

The chief chuckled. "You need to understand that Darcy loves animals, especially dogs. The ones who work with her were rescues from the Humane Society, and she trained them herself."

"How did she end up doing that?" Scott asked.

"Before we moved here from Texas, she worked as a veterinary assistant during high school. When she graduated from college, she was accepted into veterinary school. Two months into the program, my wife was diagnosed with liver cancer. Darcy left the university and took care of her mother until she died three months later." He showed Scott a framed picture of his late wife.

"I'm sorry for your loss. She was beautiful, and Darcy looks a lot like her."

The chief continued, "Darcy couldn't get another slot in veterinary school—it's harder to get into than medical school."

"What did she do?"

"She returned to the University of Texas and spent nine months earning a Master's Degree in Criminal Justice. During that time, she also took the one-month online Florida PI course and written test before applying for the PI Intern License. Then she came home to Garnet and worked under another PI in West Palm Beach for a year. Eventually, she earned her PI License and also got the Class G Concealed Firearm License."

"And she started her agency?"

"Darcy had to get the dogs and train them first. Almost two years ago, I co-signed a business loan, and she started her own private detective business. She named it Sniffers Agency - The Nose Knows."

"Clever name," Scott said.

"If she doesn't make a profit within two years, she promised me she'd give it up and apply to the Police Academy." Chief McKay frowned. "She's got two months left to show a profit before her time is up."

"Isn't her business doing well?"

"She solves every case they work, but she needs steady

jobs that pay better. Darcy takes a lot of pro-bono clients because she wants to help people who can't afford her service." The chief shook his head. "If you want to get along with my daughter, you'd better be an animal lover."

"I've always had a dog since I was a young boy." Scott shrugged. "I don't have one now because I'm away from my apartment too much. It wouldn't be fair to the dog."

The chief rubbed his chin. "Darcy has a magical way with animals. It's like she communicates with them on some special wavelength. The dogs adore her and will do anything to please her."

"Sounds like she might be a big help on that arson case," Scott said.

"By the way," the chief asked, "is my good friend, Mike Logan, your uncle?"

Scott smiled. "Yeah, Uncle Mike is the reason I moved to Florida."

"Did he tell you I was looking for a replacement for Detective Johnson?"

"It was a perfect fit because I wanted to move near my buddy, Chuck Ryan, who's one of your detectives."

"I like Chuck—good guy. How long have you been friends?"

"We met in college and have been close for years. We

even served in the same military unit." Scott paused. "Uncle Mike told me your daughter's dogs solved a missing child case. He was amazed how fast they found the kid."

Chief McKay leaned back in his swivel chair. "I remember that case. It was about a year ago." He grinned. "You'll meet the rest of my family on Friday."

"You have more children?"

"No, but they're treated like children. You'll see."

Scott stood and shook Chief McKay's hand. "I'll bring the wine Friday. Thanks for telling me all about Darcy. I'd like to be friends with her."

The Chief smiled. *Right ... friends. He'd be good for her. Seven years older. I'll give him as much help as I can.*

THREE

A Windowless Room

Kimberly feared her weird captor was getting bored with her and that he might kill her. He hadn't raped her—no violent behavior. Instead, he played games with her almost every day. He preferred chess, but they'd also played backgammon, poker, and many others. He always won.

The door lock rattled.

Her eyes widened as a tall man wearing a skeleton mask and an expensive suit entered carrying a white lace gown. He dropped it on her lap. "Put this on." He tugged on his French cuffs and adjusted his ruby cuff links.

She slid off the bed and carried the gown to the bathroom.

"Hurry up. It's for my photo gallery."

A few minutes later, she returned wearing the wedding gown.

"Good, now stand next to the painting I just hung on that wall and smile." He held up a cellphone.

Kimberly smoothed her blond hair and faked a smile, terrified this would be her final act.

Her masked captor snapped some pictures and then checked them. "These turned out great. Keep that dress on. I'll be back later for our game." He turned and left.

The door lock clicked.

She glanced at her left ankle, sore from a metal cuff connected to a long, heavy chain anchored to the iron bedframe.

"This might be my last day. I've got to get out of here, but how?" she muttered to herself.

She surveyed her prison—a ten-foot-square room with an adjoining bathroom, no windows, and one locked door leading into a hallway.

"It looks the same as it has every day since I first arrived here about four months ago." She prayed, "God, please help me."

She closed her eyes.

Stop feeling hopeless. Think. I've read lots of mystery novels. Must be something here that can help me.

She focused on "The Face of War," a macabre painting by Salvador Dali depicting a skeleton head with the eye sockets and mouth filled with more skeleton heads. It was the picture she'd posed beside on the wall.

The mounting wire!

She leaped from the bed and lifted the painting off the wall. Sucking in her breath, she turned it over and found a wire stretched across the back.

"Yes!" She carried the painting to her bed, sat with it on her lap, and unwound one end of the wire from where it was wrapped around itself near the eye loop.

The sharp tip on the wire punctured her finger, and blood dripped onto the back of the valuable canvas and onto her white dress. She wiped her bleeding finger on the bed sheet and kept working. In a few more seconds, she had the wire free of the frame.

With the wire bent over itself into a stiff lock pick, she went to work. After fumbling with many failed attempts, she heard a crisp click, and her ankle cuff fell away.

She yanked the wire out of the ankle lock and rushed to the metal door. Tilting her head, she tried to see into the tiny hole as she inserted the wire.

The lock clicked, and the door slammed into her, knocking her to the floor.

The man in the skeleton mask yanked her up and threw her onto the bed. He snatched up the ankle cuff.

"Clever girl! None of the others ever managed *this*." He clamped the cuff to her ankle. "Sit still." He grabbed the wire and shook a finger at her. "You don't want to make me angry."

Kimberly faced the menacing man. His sinister eyes, exposed through the skeleton mask, radiated a murderous lust that filled her with terror.

She scooted back against the backboard and hugged herself, her eyes watering and her body trembling.

"This won't do." He pointed at the bloody dress and sheet. "Get into the shower while I arrange for clean sheets and a change of clothes." He grabbed her arm and yanked her from the bed. "Go." He shoved her toward the bathroom.

Terrified, she turned on the shower and stepped inside, taking her time. When she finished stripping and washing, she wrapped a towel around herself and peeked into the bedroom.

Fresh sheets covered her bed, and a clean dress and

underwear were draped across it.

Kimberly eased into the room and glanced around. Her captor wasn't there.

She dressed quickly and hung the wet gown and towel in the bathroom after using the towel to dry off the chain.

Dali's creepy painting was gone and a different painting was on the wall. She checked behind it. A heavy string stretched between the mounting eyelets. Tears ran down her cheeks as she slumped on the edge of the bed.

The door swung open, and the masked man entered.

"Good, you're clean and dressed." He gestured to a chair. "Ready for another game?"

He placed a checker board on a small table bordered by two chairs. "This should be easier for you. Chess isn't your game."

She sat in the chair and glanced at the round game pieces.

"Red or black?" He pointed at the checkers.

"Red," she said in a weak voice.

"Good choice." He arranged the checkers on the board. "Remember, if you win this game, you get to go home, but if you lose, you're stuck here with me until you win one." He waved at the red checkers. "Your move."

"I'll do my best." Kimberly managed to take one of his

black checkers on her first move. As the game progressed, she continued to hold a small lead.

He made his moves quickly, sometimes making errors that benefitted her.

Unnerved by his creepy skeleton mask, she barely managed the courage to ask, "Will you really let me go if I win?" She took another black checker.

"My dear, I always keep my promises." His next move took one of her red checkers, leaving him behind by two. "Your move."

Kimberly's final move won the game, leaving her wondering if the win had been too easy, especially after months of losing every kind of game they'd played.

He kissed her hand. "Well done, my dear. I knew you could do it." He glanced at his gold Patek Philippe watch. "We'll enjoy a celebratory dinner, and then I'll take you home." He stood. "I'll return with our meal in an hour. While you're waiting, why don't you fix your hair so you'll look nice for your homecoming?" He left the room and locked the door.

Am I really going home? I sure hope so. I miss my family.

She brushed her long blond hair and pulled it into a ponytail.

It wasn't long before her captor arrived with a dinner tray. She joined him at the table.

"I brought one of my favorite vintage wines." He poured red wine into her glass. "I hope you like Chateau Lafite Rothschild. It will pair nicely with this Chateaubriand Bearnaise for two."

He paused. "Try the wine."

She took a generous sip, set the glass down, and smiled. "It tastes wonderful."

"I'm glad you like it." He motioned toward her glass. "Drink your fill. We have plenty."

She took a deep drink, savoring the smooth wine with a hint of almond. Then she leaned back against the chair and closed her eyes.

Forever.

* * *

He smiled at Kimberly's corpse, her lips blue with a bit of foaming at her nose and mouth. The killer left the room and sauntered down the narrow basement corridor to a small office at the end of the hallway. He pulled off his mask and hung it on a hook, then sat in a leather executive chair and leaned back, smiling.

Every time another blonde dies, I feel almost as good as I did when I killed my mother and sister. Blondes are so evil.

FOUR

The McKay Ranch

Darcy was busy setting the table for dinner when her dad came home.

He asked, "What did you think of Detective Scott Logan?"

"He's arrogant and bossy. *And* he probably thinks he's God's gift to women because he's handsome." She jutted out her chin. "Well, he doesn't impress me."

"Geez," Joe said, taken aback by her scathing comments. "All of the men in my department think he's a great guy, and I like him. Honey, Scott needs your help with a case I assigned him. He's replacing Johnson, who retired last week."

"Oh, I see you're on a first name basis already."

"Aw, give the guy a chance." He put his hands on her shoulders and looked into her eyes. "Knowing what a fine upstanding citizen you are, I told him you'd help with his case." He hesitated. "And I invited him to dinner Friday."

Her eyes widened. "*What*?"

He held his hands up and kissed the tip of her nose. "I'll do all the shopping and cooking. And I'll make my famous barbequed ribs."

She heaved a big sigh. "I didn't want to work with him, but since you two are buddies now, I'll try to be nice."

He put his arm around her shoulder. "Thanks, sweetheart. Now we need to talk about your business loan. Do you have the money to make the bank payment this month?"

"Don't worry, Dad. I've got most of it, and I'm expecting a check soon."

"Remember our agreement. If you don't earn a profit within two years, you'll enroll in the Police Academy and then join the Garnet Police. I know you've had a hard time making the loan payments every month, and you haven't even covered all your costs, have you?"

Darcy's face reddened as she stared at the floor. "Well,

no, not yet, but I love my work and my dogs. And I really appreciate the financial help you've given me, Dad. I promise I'll pay back every penny once my business is in the black."

"Honey, our family has been in law enforcement for three generations.   You've got the skills and instincts for police work, and I know you'd excel at it."

"I understand how you feel, Dad, but you have to admit my agency helps the police a lot. I'll keep my word if I don't show a profit in the next two months."

She hugged him and finished setting the table.

FIVE

Friday evening, Chief Joe McKay drove home to his secluded ranch, and Detective Scott Logan followed him. The road ended at the edge of a forest, and Joe turned left into a long driveway that bordered the trees. He parked next to a red barn near a brick ranch-style house with an attached two-car garage. Scott parked beside his car. The sound of barking dogs carried from the house.

Joe said, "This area is home to farms, ranches, and people who want more acreage." He pointed at a dense forest beyond his pasture. "Over there's the Florida Wildlife Refuge."

Scott glanced around. "This looks like a nice, peaceful place to live."

Joe nodded, opening his trunk. "Will you help me stack these bags of dog food in the barn?"

"Sure, I'm right behind you." Scott picked up a couple of sacks and followed Chief McKay into the barn. He noticed a row of cages that held a menagerie of wild animals. A red fox with a bandaged paw caught his attention. He peered into the cage. "I've never seen a fox this close. He's a handsome little guy."

"Darcy found him starving in the forest with his paw caught in a trap. She'll return him to the wild when he's able to hunt on his own."

"You must lead an interesting life here."

Joe chuckled. "Interesting isn't exactly the word I'd use."

Scott stopped at his car to grab the bottle of wine and then followed Joe into the house. A pack of dogs rushed at him. They slid across the white-tiled kitchen floor and shoved him against the wall.

"Hey, there, halt the assault. I've been invited," Scott said in a firm tone.

The chief laughed. "I hope you don't mind letting our ranch security team perform their duties." Joe took the wine from him, set the bottle on the kitchen counter, and turned to the dogs.

Scott shrugged and ran his hand through his thick, dark hair. "I don't mind if it'll put them at ease. What do you want me to do?"

"Stand in the middle of the kitchen with your legs apart and hold your arms straight out at your sides."

The dogs backed up and stood in line facing Scott.

"Is this going to be like a pat-down, only with noses?"

"Similar." Joe turned toward a black and white Great Dane. "Guard."

The Great Dane moved in front of Scott and bared his teeth.

"Tiny guards you while the others search."

Scott raised his eyebrows. "This giant dog's name is *Tiny*?"

"It's a ridiculous name for him, but Darcy says he has psychological issues about his size, so she named him Tiny." Joe shrugged. "He seems happy with the name."

Tiny emitted a soft woof in agreement.

The chief pointed to Scott. "Max, Dobie, search."

Dobie, a large black Doberman Pinscher, walked behind Scott and lifted Scott's jacket with his nose to check for a gun. Not finding one, he looked at Tiny, gave one bark, went back in line, and sat.

"Good boy, Dobie," Joe said.

Max, a honey-colored German shepherd, sniffed the front of Scott's body from his shoes to his waist. Then he stood on his hind legs and put his paws on Scott's shoulders, forcing Scott to take a step backward to keep his balance. Max nosed inside Scott's open jacket and took his handgun from his shoulder holster, gave it to Joe, sat at the head of the line, and barked once.

"Good boy, Max." He turned to the Labrador retriever. "Laddie, search."

Laddie, a yellow Lab, sniffed the sides of Scott's body from his ankles to his pants pockets.

Scott grinned at his chief of police. "This is quite a production."

Laddie slid his muzzle into Scott's right back pocket and deftly removed his wallet. He brought it to Joe, gave Scott a backward glance, sat down in line, and barked once.

"Thank you, Laddie, well done."

Scott was impressed. "He'd make a good pick-pocket. I didn't feel him take it." Scott lowered his arms.

Tiny growled.

Scott jerked his arms back up and shook his head. "That was well executed. I'd like to shake their hands, eh paws."

Joe commanded, "Shake hands."

Scott went down the line of dogs, shaking their paws and praising each one by name.

"What about me? Don't I get any recognition?"

Scott glanced at the kitchen door when he heard Darcy's voice. She wasn't there.

"Well, say something!"

Scott turned toward the sound and spotted an African grey parrot on a perch by the kitchen window. The parrot had imitated Darcy's voice perfectly.

"I'm sorry, Sylvester, please accept my apology," Joe said.

"Apology accepted, but don't let it happen again," the parrot said, ruffling his feathers.

Joe glanced at his guest and waved at the parrot. "Scott, meet Sylvester. He's the oldest member of our family."

"And the wisest," the parrot said.

"I'm pleased to meet you, Sylvester." Scott's blue eyes twinkled as he smiled.

"I should think so. You seldom get a chance to meet an intelligent parrot like me."

Joe held up his hands. "What can I say? We have a crazy family. Come on, I'll pour some beer in ice-cold mugs and warm up the grill. Darcy should be home soon." He switched off the parrot's personal TV on the kitchen counter. It kept the bird amused when they weren't home.

Sylvester hopped onto Joe's shoulder as he led the way, and the dogs followed them through a large screened pool area to the outside patio. They walked under an arched trellis covered with bougainvillea vines forming a mass of maroon blossoms.

"Won't Sylvester fly away?" Scott asked.

"Why would I fly away?" The sarcastic bird flapped his wings. "I'm the head honcho here, and it's a jungle out there."

"Sometimes we hear lions roar at the Big Cats Sanctuary nearby," Joe said. "They have twenty lions and tigers."

Scents of jasmine hung in the air, carried by the flowers covering the fence around the patio. Sylvester landed on the top of a chair under a big shade umbrella. Joe filled two large frosted mugs with beer and then joined Scott on comfortable chairs under the umbrella table near the built-in brick grill.

"This is quite a place you have here, Chief."

"We enjoy it, especially after a hectic day at work."

Scott sipped his beer. "I hope Darcy can help me find

the arsonist who's been setting fires in those vacant homes. I'm worried someone will get hurt. Teenagers break into the empty houses to hold parties, and no one can see them through the boarded windows."

"Her dogs will find the arsonist. They're trained to detect all kinds of scents. Did you know humans only have about five million olfactory cells, but a dog has two hundred million?"

"That's incredible," Scott said.

As they waited for Darcy, they enjoyed sharing stories about their work in law enforcement.

SIX

When the dogs barked, Scott turned and spotted Darcy's white Chevy Suburban coming up the long driveway.

Joe stood. "Time to cook. I'll get the ribs out of the refrigerator. Relax and enjoy your beer."

The dogs ran over to greet Darcy, and Scott walked toward her as she petted them.

He smiled and said in a sincere tone, "Please accept my apology for the misunderstanding the other day. How did it go at the animal hospital? Is the dachshund going to be okay?"

Darcy smiled. "Apology accepted. My veterinarian friend, Andy, wants to keep her for a few days. He told me she has a cracked rib and deep bruises. Daisy has been his patient for a few years. He told me the bully's wife brought her in for shots before she died last year, and he noticed bruises on the wife too." Darcy said under her breath, "That brute had better hope he never crosses my path again."

Scott nodded. "Do you think you can find a good home for the dog?"

"I already have. I'm going to keep her when Andy releases her. He told me she's been spayed. My dogs are all neutered, so I think they'll get along with her."

"That's kind of you. Your dad had the dogs demonstrate how they search a suspect. They're amazing."

Darcy smiled. "Thank you. I'll be right back. I'm going to get a glass of iced tea. Would you like one?"

"No, thank you, I'm still working on the beer your dad gave me." Scott walked back to the table and found his mug empty. He held it up and shouted, "Darcy, looks like I need a refill."

She nodded and waved before she entered the house.

Soon the chief was busy grilling barbequed ribs and corn cobs wrapped in foil. When he had everything set up, he reached for his beer mug. It was empty. "Scott, will you keep an eye on the grill while I get another beer?"

"Sure, it smells delicious." He turned the ribs over and glanced at the dogs. All of them, except Tiny, were alert with their noses in the air, sniffing the mouth-watering aroma. Tiny was on his back with his legs up in the air, snoring.

Joe wheeled a large two-shelved cart with one hand while holding a beer bottle in his other hand. The cart was stacked with everything they needed for dinner, including the dogs' dishes and their food. Darcy walked beside Joe, holding a glass of iced tea and a bottle of beer.

As the chief poured beer into his mug, he said, "I can't understand what happened to my first beer. I'm sure I didn't drink it all."

When Tiny heard the cart roll onto the patio, he woke up and belched.

"Uh oh, Tiny must've been at it again." Darcy put her glass on the table.

"I should've known." Joe shook his head. "He drank my beer when I wasn't looking."

Scott grinned. "That must be what happened to mine too. Is he drunk?"

Darcy sighed. "Yes, and he gets all lovey-dovey from the alcohol. He'll want to sit on my lap and lick my face, but I'm too small to hold a Great Dane. I'm going to have to sit where my lap is unavailable or stand the rest of the night."

Scott couldn't get the image out of his head and burst out laughing.

"Sure, it's funny to you," she said. "You aren't the one who might get crushed by a giant dog."

Tiny focused his eyes on Darcy and weaved his way to her. She quickly sat in a chair and scooted it under the table. He stood behind her, plopped his big head on her shoulder, sighed, and licked her cheek.

"See what I mean?" she said.

As they enjoyed dinner, Scott heaped praise on Chief McKay and Darcy for the delicious meal. The dogs waited patiently for the table scraps to be mixed in with their dog food.

After everyone had been fed, including Sylvester, and things were put away, Joe excused himself. He settled in the living room and watched television.

Darcy and Scott relaxed outside on the screened patio with glasses of wine from the bottle Scott had brought.

He told her about the fires the arsonist had set in the Regal Palms housing development. "A five-gallon gasoline can was found near one of the torched houses, but we couldn't get any fingerprints off it. The fire chief said some arsonists like to mingle in the crowd and watch the fires they set. Do you think your dogs would be able to find the arsonist if he were in the crowd?"

Darcy nodded. "If he's there, he'll still have the scent of gasoline on him, and my dogs will find him."

"Will you help me investigate the next fire? We've been fortunate no one has been injured so far, but the odds are against us. The abandoned homes are too inviting for teenagers to break into for parties."

Darcy nodded. "Of course, we'll help you."

"I've been authorized to hire your agency. You can give me the bill, or give it to your dad, whichever you prefer." He smiled. "You must have interesting stories to tell about your searches and rescues."

"My furry employees have found lost humans, animals, jewelry, and numerous other things. They've also searched for drugs, weapons, explosives, and cadavers."

"Your dad told me about their uncanny sense of smell. I feel like I've known Joe a long time. I hope you and I can be friends too." He smiled as he gazed into her emerald-green eyes.

Darcy felt drawn to his masculine magnetism and self-confidence. She stiffened, not wanting to be dazzled by his manly charm. Besides, he was too handsome to be true to one woman. She'd dated men like him before. Big mistakes.

She smiled. "Time will tell."

Scott asked, "Do the dogs always bark when a car drives up to the house?"

"No, they only bark at my car and Dad's because they recognize the sounds and want to greet us. No one else would know we have dogs."

"I'm impressed."

"You should be. Only people with good intentions get past our ranch security team."

"Glad to see the dogs and you recognized my good intentions."

Darcy arched a brow. "You got a free pass tonight, but consider yourself on probation."

SEVEN

A few days later, around four in the afternoon, Scott called Darcy. "The fire department just called me. They have another foreclosed house on fire. It's at 420 Azalea Avenue in the Regal Palms development. Can you bring the dogs?"

"Yes, we'll leave in five minutes. Tell the first responders my dogs will be wearing blue bandanas. I'll meet you near the burning house."

"Okay, you're the boss."

"That's right."

"I'll be waiting for you."

Darcy petted the newest member of their family. "Daisy, you stay here with Sylvester while we go to work.

Good girl."

She glanced at the parrot. "I'm counting on you to look after her while we're gone. She's had a rough life, and I want her to feel welcome and safe here."

"Don't worry. She loves to watch TV with me, and she's been getting along great with the big boys. I think Laddie is in love with her."

"That's sweet. We'll be back in a couple hours." Darcy gathered her team, tied on their blue bandanas, and loaded them into the white SUV.

* * *

A crowd had gathered around the fire, and police officers kept them back. Scott instructed the cops on the scene to be on the lookout for a Labrador, Doberman, German shepherd, and Great Dane wearing blue bandanas. He said, "Don't hinder the dogs. Give them full access to the area near the fire. They're coming to search for the arsonist."

Scott moved behind the crowd and waited for Darcy. When she arrived, the four dogs jumped out of the SUV and eagerly waited for her orders. She and her team followed Scott and stopped a short distance from the burning house. The dogs knew their bandanas meant they were expected to work.

Scott handed her an empty five-gallon gasoline can found outside the burning house.

Darcy held the can under the dogs' noses. "Take scent." After they sniffed the can, Darcy commanded, "Search and hold."

The dogs raced into the crowd, and Scott and Darcy followed.

The spectators didn't notice the four dogs moving silently among them, searching for the scent of gasoline. Max was the first to smell it on the arsonist's shoes. He sat in front of the man and waited for his partners. Dobie came and sat by the man's right leg, and Laddie sat by his left leg. Tiny stood behind the man.

After they were all in position, Max gave a sharp bark. The arsonist looked down at him, tried to evade him, and bumped into growling Laddie. The man tried to maneuver away and side-stepped into snarling Dobie. Max bared his fangs, and the man backed up, turned to get away, and faced Tiny. He let out a cry of terror when the big Great Dane bared his fangs. He froze, surrounded by four ferocious dogs, and shouted, "Help!"

Darcy heard Max bark as she pushed her way through

the crowd with Scott right behind her. People standing near the frightened man quickly moved away when they saw the four big dogs.

Scott handcuffed the terrified man. "I'm arresting you on suspicion of arson." He read the man his rights and led him to a police car with the dogs and Darcy following.

When the patrol car pulled away, Scott said, "Thank you, Darcy. Without your dogs' help, that guy wouldn't have been caught."

Darcy smiled. "You're welcome."

He leaned over to pet the dogs. "Great work, guys. I knew you could do it. I'm buying each of you a box of dog biscuits."

"How did you know that's what I always give them after they complete a job?"

"I didn't. That's what I gave my dogs. Hey, we've got to celebrate this. Let me take you and your dad out to dinner tonight—nothing fancy, just good food."

She was caught up by his enthusiasm and knew her dad would be pleased. "Okay. What time?"

"That's up to you." He glanced at the squad car pulling away with the arsonist locked in the back seat.

She looked at her watch. "It's five-thirty now. We can be ready to go in an hour and a half."

"Okay. I'll pick you up at seven." He walked with her and the dogs back to her vehicle and waved as she drove away.

Happy, he whistled on the way back to his car. *I think she's warming up to me.*

EIGHT

A Windowless Room

"That's right." The man wearing a skeleton mask waved to one side. "Stand closer to the painting. You look lovely in that wedding gown."

He snapped several pictures with his cellphone and checked them. "These turned out great. You'll be a perfect addition to my photo gallery." He pulled out a chair. "Have a seat and we'll play our game. You're a much better chess player than my last guest," he said. "I'd better be careful, or you might win this one. Then I'd have to let you go."

A beautiful blonde about twenty years old lifted a

shaky hand and moved her pawn across the chessboard. "Will you really let me go if I win?"

"Of course. I'm a man of my word." His sinister eyes gleamed from inside his macabre mask as he blocked her knight.

She glanced at the disturbing painting she'd posed beside. It was on the wall by their table, and she noted the faint signature. "Is that a real Salvador Dali painting?"

He nodded. "The Face of War." He grinned through his frightening mask. "Appropriate, don't you agree?"

"You mean because it's a skeleton face, kind of like your mask?"

"I find the similarities interesting." He waved his hand at the board. "Your move."

Her eyes brightened as she made the decisive move. "Checkmate."

He sat back and studied the board. "Well done, my dear. I didn't see that coming. Looks like your six-month stay here has come to an end. We'll enjoy one last dinner together, and then I'll take you home."

"How far is it from here?" she asked, hoping he was telling the truth.

"It'll be about a three-hour flight in my private jet. I'll call my pilots and have them get the plane ready to go."

He left and locked the door.

An hour later, he returned with a dinner tray. He pulled the cork on a bottle of French Chardonnay. "This delightful wine will complement the chicken cordon bleu were having." He filled her glass. "Try it."

She lifted the wine glass and took a deep drink. "It's good. I taste a hint of almonds." She set down the glass, leaned her head against the chair back, and gasped. Her eyes widened, and her lips turned blue. Foam bubbled around her mouth and nose. She stared at the masked man with her soft brown eyes locked open in terror.

Forever.

* * *

He leaned back in the wingback chair and adjusted his ruby cuff links. Smiling at the blond corpse, he said, "This one is dedicated to you, sister dear. Unlike my endless losses with you, here I never lose until it's time for you to die again. I consider that a win too." He took in a deep breath and exhaled. "Ah, Sybil, it gives me great pleasure to imagine I'm killing you over and over. I also take great comfort in knowing you'll never rest in peace."

The man in the mask stood and strode to the door. He

opened it, turned, and took one last look at the dead girl.

Blondes truly are evil—every last one of them.

NINE

The McKay Ranch

Scott arrived at the ranch and parked in the driveway. He reached across the seat for a big bag holding a box of fine chocolates, a six-pack of Joe's favorite beer, and four boxes of dog biscuits. "Darn, I forgot to get something for Sylvester," he said to himself.

He reached in his car's glove compartment for a package of cheddar crackers he kept there in case he got hungry while working surveillance. "I hope that old saying, 'Polly wants a cracker,' is true."

He rang the doorbell and heard Sylvester shout, "Scott's here with a bag. Could be goodies. Let him in."

Chief McKay opened the door. "Sylvester can see you through the kitchen window. He's our official announcer."

Scott pulled out the six-pack and handed it to Joe. "This is just a small token of my appreciation for that delicious dinner Friday."

"Thanks, but this is too much. You're taking us to dinner."

"No restaurant can serve a meal as delicious as yours, Chief." Scott set the boxes of dog biscuits on the kitchen counter. "I promised the guys a reward for their amazing work finding the arsonist. The perp admitted setting the fires to get back at the banks for foreclosing on his house and on some of his friends' homes. I can understand his frustration, but I don't think he realized he might've injured or killed someone."

Daisy wagged her little tail and trotted up to Scott.

"Hey, is this the dog Darcy rescued from that drunk?" Scott petted her.

"Yep, Daisy is part of our family now." Joe petted her head. "She's settling in nicely. The big dogs love her, and Darcy has already started training her."

Scott glanced around. "Where *are* the big dogs?"

"They're with Darcy. She's almost ready."

Scott sucked in a deep breath when Darcy walked in

dressed in a sleek green dress the color of her eyes. She stood a little taller in matching stilettos, and her long red hair fell in soft waves over her shoulders and down her back.

Scott's well-muscled body moved with easy grace as he stepped forward and gave her the fancy box of candy. "You look lovely. I hope you like this brand of chocolates." He smiled sincerely, and his teeth looked strikingly white in contrast to his handsome tanned face.

"Thank you for the compliment and the candy. It's my favorite brand." Darcy turned and put the chocolates on the kitchen counter. *You can tone down the charm, handsome. I'm not letting myself get involved with you.*

"I didn't know Daisy was here, or I would've brought some tiny dog biscuits for her." He reached into his pocket and gave Joe a handful of wrapped crackers. "These are for Sylvester."

"Thank you, Scott," Sylvester said. "Chief, please put our favorite cop show on TV in the living room and unwrap the crackers. I'll record the show so you can view it later."

"Okay, but skip the commercials." Joe tore off the clear wrappers.

"But the family's favorite commercial is the dog

driving the car to the beach with his friends. Max always wants a replay."

"Okay." Joe sighed and carried Sylvester to his perch in the living room.

Scott grinned. "Sylvester is quite a character. Does he always boss around everyone in the house?"

Darcy nodded. "He has a huge ego and thinks he's the master of our world. I'd describe him as an intelligent can opener with an attitude."

Scott laughed at the description and was still smiling as they walked to the car. He opened the front passenger door for Darcy before she could maneuver into the back seat. The chief sat behind her, and they were on their way.

It was quiet in the car until Scott asked, "How long have you had your business, Darcy?"

"Almost two years. How long have you been a detective?"

"Two years in Dallas, one year in Chicago, and a little over a week here," Scott said. "When Uncle Mike told me about a detective retiring here, I jumped at the chance to live in sunny Florida near my good friend, Chuck Ryan."

"I know Chuck," she said. "He's nice. All my girlfriends like him."

"We've been friends since college—even served

together in the military."

"I guess you're glad you moved to Florida."

He nodded. "It's working out well."

"You managed to discover one of our favorite restaurants. Do you eat out often?" Joe asked.

"Yeah, I get tired of frozen dinners and canned food." Scott parked the car, and they walked into the restaurant.

They were escorted to a table, and Scott ordered a bottle of wine while they waited for their dinner.

He noticed Darcy's delicate hands and manicured nails as she held her glass. "I'm surprised you can keep your fingernails so nice with all the work you do around the ranch."

She set her glass down, held her hands in front of her, and smiled. "Ah, yes. These are stick-on nails. I only wear them on special occasions because I find it difficult to pick up small objects when I wear them."

His blue eyes twinkled as his gaze searched her eyes. "I'm glad you think this is a special occasion."

"Any time I'm invited out is a special occasion for me. Just as it is when I go dancing with my friends or to dinner and other places." She attempted to seem nonchalant.

About halfway through their dinner, Scott asked,

"How's your food?"

Joe said, "My steak is delicious. How's yours?"

"It's okay, but not as good as the barbequed ribs at your cookout. Darcy, how's your salmon?"

"Delicious, thank you. It's always nice to dine out with friends and family."

"The chief told me you have a magical way with your dogs and can get them to do anything you ask."

"Dad exaggerates my talents." She playfully nudged her father. "After all, dogs are human too."

Scott raised a brow.

"Okay, I tend to think of them as furry humans. They have an amazing ability to sense what you're thinking and to know your intentions. And they can spot a phony instantly," she said.

Scott said, "I agree."

When they finished their leisurely dinner, Scott checked his watch and glanced at Joe and Darcy. "Is there another place you'd like to go? It's only nine thirty."

The chief looked at his daughter for a clue how to answer.

"Thank you, but it's been a long day, and I have a lot of work to do tomorrow. You can drop me off if you and Dad want to go someplace else."

"No, I'm tired," Joe said. "Let's call it a night."

When they arrived at the ranch, Chief McKay thanked Scott for dinner, hurried to the house, unlocked the door, and went inside.

Darcy frowned. *Dad, don't play matchmaker.*

Scott opened the car door for Darcy and walked her to the house. "I'd like to take you to lunch tomorrow when I pick up the bill for your agency's services. After all, you need to keep up your strength to kick giant dog abusers."

"I'll have to check my schedule. Call me tomorrow." She took his hand and quickly moved to the step above him. "Thanks for dinner."

His eyes twinkled as he kissed her hand. "Sweet dreams."

Catching the scent of his after-shave on her hand when she withdrew it, she said, "Goodnight," and hurried inside.

When she closed the door, the dogs surrounded her, wanting to be petted.

"Tell us all about it, Darcy. Was it a good dinner?" Sylvester asked.

She yawned. "Dinner was delicious. I'm going to bed. Good night all."

Joe gave her a hug. "I'll turn in after Sylvester and I

watch my favorite cop show." He glanced at the parrot. "I hope you remembered to record it."

"Always, Chief." The bird settled on his perch beside the recliner. "Don't forget my crackers."

The dogs gathered around the TV to watch the show again before they took their regular places on guard duty for the night.

TEN

The next morning, Darcy checked her cellphone and realized she'd forgotten to recharge it the previous night. She plugged it in by the toaster and took the sleep cover off Sylvester's cage.

When she opened the tiny wire door, he sailed to his perch by the window and surveyed his domain like a king. "What are your plans for today, Darcy?"

"My usual chores. What about you?"

"I'll watch my favorite soap opera and see if Nancy discovers Jim is cheating on her with her best friend, Carol. Then I'll watch some game shows and my favorite cop series."

Hands on her hips, she looked at him. "I hope you

realize what a great life you have here."

He puffed out his feathers and squawked, "Have you forgotten I'm head of ranch security? I keep a sharp eye on things when you and the chief aren't home."

She held up her hands. "Yes, you do."

After cleaning his cage, she lined the bottom with papers, then washed and refilled all his food and water cups. She switched on his television set, peeled a banana, and held out half of it so he could eat it.

He tilted his head and gave her the one-eyed bird stare, squawked thank you, and went at the banana like a hungry teenager.

After she ate breakfast and fed the dogs, she went to the barn and fed the injured animals that were temporarily locked in cages.

Darcy reached into a big box and scooped up a darling kitten with one black ear and one white ear. Elderly Mrs. Abernathy had chosen it from the barn cat's litter. She put it in the pet carrier and planned to give it a bath before delivering it to its new home.

She set the carrier down near an outside faucet that had a hose and spray nozzle attached and went back into the barn to get the pet shampoo and a towel. When she returned, she noticed the dogs sniffing the empty carrier and its open door.

"Oh, no." She snatched up the carrier, looked behind the barn, and spotted the frightened kitten running under the back fence into the pasture. When she lunged to grab the kitten, it climbed up a huge tree near the gate.

Darcy pointed at the dogs. "Stay." She ran to the tree. Setting aside the pet carrier, she said, "Here, kitty, kitty. It's okay. The big doggies won't hurt you. Come down, kitty."

The kitten climbed higher.

Groaning, she said, "Darn it, this isn't working."

She returned to the dogs. "Come. I need a ladder to get the kitty down."

She went back to the barn and dragged a sixteen-foot ladder through the gate to the tree. The dogs watched her struggle, leaning the heavy old wooden ladder up against the big oak. She paused a moment to catch her breath and then climbed up to the top rung. She clutched the tree with one arm and tried to grab a branch that was almost within reach.

The shift in her weight made the ladder slide sideways. Lunging forward, she grabbed a bough with both hands, her peasant blouse slipping out of her waistband.

The ladder crashed to the ground and broke apart as she swung her legs up, wrapped them around the stout branch, pulled herself into a sitting position, and tucked her blouse back into her jeans.

She glanced up the kitten. "This is a fine mess you've gotten me into, and I don't have my cellphone to call for help."

The dogs stared up at her from the ground under the massive tree.

As long as I'm up here, I may as well get the kitten and try to comfort it.

She climbed higher, reached the kitten, and gently pulled it loose from its death grip on the tree.

After tucking the kitten into the front of her shirt, she worked her way down and settled in the crook of the lowest tree bough, about fifteen feet off the ground. She cradled the kitten in her arms, petting and soothing it.

ELEVEN

Scott called Darcy's cell several times and wondered why she didn't answer.

I'll take a chance on driving over there and invite her to lunch. I can be more persuasive in person.

He drove to the ranch, walked past her SUV, and rang the doorbell.

Sylvester yelled from inside the house, "There's nobody here but me. They left me all alone, Scott."

"What do you mean, no one is here? Darcy's SUV is in the driveway."

"She's outside doing chores," Sylvester said.

Maybe she's in the barn.

He walked toward it and spotted the ranch security

team running in his direction.

He asked, "Where's Darcy?"

Max took Scott's wrist gently in his mouth and pulled him toward the pasture behind the barn.

"Okay, okay, I know what you want. I'm coming."

Tiny walked behind Scott, nudging him along with his head. Dobie led the way with Laddie following. When he was under the tree, Max let go of his wrist, sat down, and looked up into the tree with the rest of the dogs.

Scott gazed up and grinned. "Well, well, well. What kind of bird is that? I believe it's a redheaded tree sitter, quite rare in this part of Florida."

Darcy frowned. "Now that you've made your witty remark, do you have any ideas how to get me and the kitten down without a ladder? That broken one on the ground is the only one we have."

The sky darkened, and thunder rumbled in the distance.

Scott pointed at the pet carrier. "I assume that's meant for the kitten you're holding. Drop her down to me. I promise I'll catch her."

"Okay, but make sure you lock the carrier door. It didn't fasten properly, and that's how this mess started."

"I'm ready." He held out his hands. "Drop her."

She let the kitten fall into Scott's waiting hands.

The frightened cat scratched him, but he managed to put it in the carrier and secure the door.

He tilted his head back. "Okay, now wrap your arms around that bough you're sitting on and then let your body swing down. Let go when I tell you. I'll wait while you get in position."

She grabbed the branch and let her legs drop down. Her peasant blouse pulled out of her waistband again as she hung below the bough.

He raised his arms up. "Okay, let go."

Her blouse billowed out as she dropped, and it covered his head when he caught her.

He froze with his head stuck under her blouse.

I'm in big trouble. What do I do now?

His face was pressed against her pounding heart with his nose trapped between her bra-covered breasts.

In a strained voice she said, "Lift me up so I can free my blouse from around your head."

He lifted her, and she tugged up on her blouse.

"Ouch! My ear almost came off with your shirt."

"Sorry," she said. "I was in a hurry."

He lowered her body until they faced each other. Her flushed face telegraphed her embarrassment.

She feels so soft in my arms.

Darcy snapped, "Put me down!"

He dismissed the thought of letting her slide farther down his body and held her away from him as he gently set her down.

Lightning flashed, followed a second later by booming thunder.

She shoved her blouse into her jeans and grabbed the pet carrier. "Better hurry."

They sprinted to the barn as it began to rain. Light sprinkles became a heavy downpour just as they entered the safety of the barn.

She avoided eye contact with him as she put the kitten back in with the rest of its litter.

He stood beside her. "Thunderstorms like this usually don't last long. We can still go to lunch in a little while."

She glanced up at him, still blushing. "You go. I ... I'm not hungry, and anyway, I haven't prepared my bill for the city yet. My dad can bring it in tomorrow."

He arched a brow. "You need nourishment so you can kick bullies and climb huge trees. Besides, how can you refuse me after my gallant rescue?" His gaze wandered from her eyes to the rest of her body.

"You've got some nerve." She punched him in the arm.

"Ouch! Why'd you do that?"

She crossed her arms. "You *leered* at me."

"It was just an admiring glance—a male reflex." He rubbed his arm.

She glared at him. "Oh, yeah? You'd better curb your male reflexes, or I'll change that deep, sensual voice of yours into a falsetto."

His jaw dropped as he considered what she'd said. Focusing on the positive, he asked, "You really think I have a deep, sensual voice?"

She rolled her eyes. "*Unbelievable*! That's the only thing you heard?"

He grinned. "Seemed like the most important."

The lively twinkle in his eyes fueled her anger.

The dogs watched them, turning their heads from Darcy to Scott as each spoke.

She stamped her foot. "You, you, you're impossible." She turned and ran through the pouring rain to the house with the dogs at her heels.

Scott heaved a deep sigh. *I wonder how long it'll take her to cool down this time. I'd better proceed with caution around this fiery redhead.* He glanced at his watch. *The chief should be having lunch about now. I'll join him and get his advice.* Scott ran to his car and drove to town.

The rain had stopped by the time he parked in front of Sally's Diner. He went inside and found Darcy's dad sitting in a booth. "Hey, Chief, do you mind if I join you?"

Chief McKay wiped his mouth with a napkin. "Have a seat. I thought you were having lunch with Darcy."

"That was my plan, but things didn't work out. You won't believe what happened."

"When it comes to my family, as crazy as anything sounds, I've learned to be a believer." Joe laid his napkin on his lap and took a sip of coffee. "Fill me in and don't skip any details."

Joe continued to eat as he listened to Scott's tale of woe. He choked on a mouthful of food when Scott came to the part about Darcy's blouse stuck on his head.

The chief reached for a glass of water, grinned, and shook his head. "It's a good thing she likes you. She punched you instead of kicking you like she kicked that guy who hurt the little dog. Give her some time to simmer down. If that doesn't work, I'll invite you over for another cookout."

"Thanks, Chief, I knew you'd understand." Scott leaned forward and frowned. "Are you *sure* she likes me? She doesn't act like it."

Joe nodded. "I'm sure. Oh, I forgot to tell you she loves to go dancing. Do you dance?"

"I wouldn't win the mirror-ball trophy on Dan*cing with the Stars*, but I might come in second or third." Scott grinned. "I worked my way through college as a dance instructor."

"That's great. Darcy also swims and enjoys most outdoor activities."

"I do too. What else can you tell me, Chief?"

"Well, let's see, she's licensed to carry a weapon, but she also has the skills to defend herself physically, as I'm sure you've observed." He smiled and glanced at his watch. "I have to get back to work. Enjoy your lunch."

"Thanks, Chief, and I appreciate the advice."

Joe stood, walked to the cash register, and smiled at Sally, the pretty dark-haired owner of the diner. "Don't forget our date Saturday night."

She returned the smile. "Forget a date with you? Never. My sister Ruth will cover for me. Now you be careful out there, handsome."

TWELVE

A Windowless Room

A petite blonde in her early twenties trembled when the door lock rattled. *Oh no, he's coming in.*

A tall, well-dressed man entered. His tailored navy silk suit and crisp white shirt with French cuffs would've made him look attractive had it not been for the skeleton mask he wore over his face. His ten-carat ruby cuff links contrasted with a white-lace wedding gown draped over his left arm.

He handed her the gown. "Put this on. I need a picture for my brides gallery."

Her hands shook so much she almost dropped the

gown as she limped to the bathroom.

"And fix your hair." He pulled out his cellphone.

When she returned dressed in the gown, he pointed at the Dali painting. "Stand beside that picture and smile."

Trembling, she thought this was the end. She tried to smile, but tears streamed down her face. "Sorry."

"What's wrong? Why are you crying?" He handed her some tissues.

"You're going to kill me now," she sobbed.

"No, my dear, I just need a nice picture before we play our daily game. Give me a smile, and then we'll play."

She dried her tears and smiled a fake smile.

"Good, that turned out fine," he said, checking the picture. "Now, have a seat." He pulled out her chair.

She sat down and set up the backgammon game he'd placed on the table.

When they rolled the dice to see who would go first, she rolled the higher number.

"You have the first roll, and don't forget—if you win, you get to go home," he said, his creepy smile showing through the mouth opening on the skeleton mask.

She rolled double sixes and was off to a good start.

As the game progressed, she maintained a small lead.

"This could be your lucky day." He paused. "What's it

been—three months?"

"I'm not sure. It's hard to keep track of time here." She took four more of her pieces off the board.

Two to go.

He rolled the dice and got a three. "Uh oh, I'm four behind you. Your roll."

She rolled double twos. "I win," she said as she moved her last two pieces off the board. "Will you let me go now?"

"Of course, but we'll have one final dinner together before I take you home. Sit tight and I'll get our meal." He closed up the game board and left.

The door lock clicked, and she exhaled a relieved sigh. *I miss my family. Will he keep his promise and take me home?*

An hour later, the masked man returned with a large meal tray and a bottle of cabernet sauvignon.

"This is a special wine from California that was aged in casks lined with almonds. It'll pair nicely with the steak Diane and steamed asparagus." He pulled out the cork and filled her glass. "Try it. It's quite tasty."

She reached out with a shaky hand and lifted the glass to her lips. After a deep sip, she put the glass down. "It's good—tastes a little like almonds." She took another drink and then leaned back against the tall chair.

A sharp intake of breath preceded her eyes closing.

Forever.

* * *

The man in the mask watched as her lips turned blue and foam bubbled out of her mouth and nose. *Hair and eyes just like my evil mother.*

"This one's for you, Mom. I sure hope you woke up right before the yacht exploded. I can only imagine your surprise when I wasn't there to die with you and my spoiled sister. Checkmate, Mommy dearest."

He stared at the dead girl in the chair. *Getting away with these murders has been too easy, and I only have one girl left to play with down here. Time to snatch a local blonde or two and watch the cops fail to catch me— such a fun game!*

THIRTEEN

The McKay Ranch

"Did you see that guy fire nine rounds from a gun that only shoots six? Geez, give me a break. We aren't *that* stupid, right, Darcy?" her dad asked.

She hadn't been paying attention to the television show they were watching after dinner and murmured, "Hmmm."

"Darcy, what's the matter? Your mind seems to be somewhere else. Do you want to watch a different program?"

"Don't change the channel. I want to see the bad guys get what they deserve," Sylvester said, mimicking Joe's voice as he sat on his special perch next to Joe's recliner. He bobbed his grey head up and down. "Quick, while the commercial's on, give me a cracker."

Darcy and Joe ignored him.

"Okay, *please* give me a cracker."

She handed him a cracker.

"Geez, you guys are sticklers for manners," the parrot grumbled.

"Dad, I need your advice."

"Sure honey, what's the matter?"

"Earlier today, I lost my temper with Scott because he embarrassed me."

He listened while Darcy told him the same story Scott had told him earlier.

"I don't think he'll ever visit us again, and I know you like him."

He searched her eyes. "Do *you* want to see him again?"

"Well ... you like him, and the family likes him, so I don't mind if you two are buddies. What should I do?"

"Wait a day or two and let things cool down. I'll come up with a plan."

"I knew you'd know what to do. Thanks, Dad." She hugged him as the late news came on.

"Give me another cracker, and I won't mention this conversation to Scott."

"Sylvester, that's blackmail. You wouldn't do that, would you?" she asked.

"*Please* give me another cracker, and I won't."

She glared at Sylvester and asked her dad, "What should I do?"

"Pay the blackmailer his cracker. If he tells Scott, I'll put him behind bars."

"Are you talking about my cage?"

"Yes, and I'll lock the door."

Darcy handed Sylvester a cracker. "You should be ashamed."

The parrot cocked his head. "It's a dirty business, but sometimes a guy's gotta do what a guy's gotta do to get by in this crazy world."

"Isn't that a quote from a movie?" Joe asked.

She frowned. "Sylvester, someday you're going to regret your manipulative ways."

"Everyone has regrets." He bobbed his head up and down. "Did I ever tell you about the time I perched on the rim of Tiny's dish while he was eating?"

"Will you two knock off the chatter?" Joe said. "I'm trying to listen to the news. There was a two-car crash not far from Lion Country Safari about an hour ago. The occupants were taken to the hospital by ambulance."

Darcy said, "I hope they're okay. If Laura's on duty, she'll see to it they get the best care."

She stretched. "I'm going to bed. Good night, Dad. I love you." She kissed his cheek, petted the dogs, and glared at Sylvester.

Ten minutes later, Joe secured the parrot in his cage and gave the dogs their nightly command, "Guard the house."

The ranch security team took their usual places for the night. Laddie lay by the glass doors to the patio, Dobie settled near the kitchen door, Tiny sat facing the front door, and Max took his position at the foot of Darcy's bed.

After putting on a nightgown, Darcy gazed out her bedroom window at the front lawn bathed in moonlight.

I bet Scott's a good kisser. She frowned. *Of course, he is—players always are.*

A cool spring breeze stirred the curtains. She breathed in the jasmine-scented fresh air circulating through the house as she slipped between the sheets.

I love the cool fresh air. It never smells like this when the A/C is on. Too bad it gets so hot and humid in the summer.

Darcy took one more glance at the moonlight filtering through her curtains before she closed her eyes.

A brief fantasy about Scott kissing me won't hurt. I'll never trust him in real life, but I may as well have a little fun in my dreams.

FOURTEEN

The next morning, Darcy headed to the barn to feed the caged animals. She stopped halfway there when her best friend, Sandy, drove up.

"What's up?" Darcy asked.

Sandy pushed her blond hair away from her pretty face. "My sister called from the hospital and told me about some people in a car crash last night."

"What happened?"

"A drunk ran into a family of three—an eight-year-old boy and his parents were injured. They're from Michigan and were on their way to Singer Island for a vacation. The father has a dislocated shoulder and bruises, the mother is unconscious with a head wound and a broken arm, and the boy has a broken leg."

"That's terrible! What about the drunk guy?"

"He didn't have any injuries, just scrapes and bruises."

Darcy shook her head. "Typical. Drunks rarely get hurt in the wrecks they cause."

"The little boy is inconsolable because his puppy is missing. Laura feels sorry for him and is worried about his dog. She loves animals as much as we do and asked if we had time to look for his dog."

Darcy glanced at her watch. "I guess I can take a look out there. I just have to feed the critters in the barn first."

"I'll help you. My sister said they're keeping the family in the hospital because the mother is still unconscious, and the boy doesn't want to go to Singer Island because he thinks he'll never see his dog again if they go farther away from the accident site."

"Do you know the puppy's breed?"

"Laura said it was a three-month-old Beagle named Barney."

"We'll need something with the dog's scent. Let's go to the hospital, meet the father and son, and see if they have a toy or something that belonged to the puppy before we start searching."

Sandy smiled and took out her cellphone. "I'll call

Laura and tell her we're coming. I knew you'd do it if you weren't busy on another case. I'll drive."

"I'll just finish taking care of the animals, and then we'll leave."

Fifteen minutes later, Darcy hopped in Sandy's car, and they drove to the hospital.

Laura, the supervisor of nurses, met them and took them to the boy's father. "Mr. Mason, this is my sister, Sandy, and our good friend, Darcy, who owns the Sniffers Agency. Her dogs do search and rescue work besides working with law enforcement, sniffing out drugs, guns, explosives, and stuff. They'll find your son's dog."

Mr. Mason's face was covered in bruises and his right arm hung in a sling. "Good to meet you."

"I'm so sorry this happened to you," Darcy said. "We'll try to find your son's dog, and there won't be any charge for my services. I just need something with Barney's scent so we can track him."

Mr. Mason smiled for the first time since the accident. "Thank you. You're all so kind." He paused. "Let me think. Barney was wearing his red coat when we left home in Michigan because it was snowing. Jimmy took it off later when we drove through warmer states. It must still be somewhere in the back seat with Barney's toys. Can you use his coat or toys to get his scent?"

"Barney's coat would be perfect," Darcy said.

He frowned. "I forgot our car was towed to the vehicle impound lot after the accident."

"That's not a problem. My dad is the police chief. I'll tell him I have your permission to get the dog's things from the back seat. Do you want your luggage too?"

"I'd hate to impose," Mr. Mason said.

"It's no bother. Do you have a key to the trunk?"

He reached into his pocket. "If you're sure it's not too much trouble, I'd love a change of clothes." Mason handed her the car keys.

"We'll stop by the police station and fill out a form to get your luggage from the vehicle impound lot," Darcy said. "May we talk to Jimmy first?"

"Of course, and thank you so much for your help. Jimmy is heartbroken."

Laura escorted them to Jimmy's room. The little boy looked up at them from his bed, his eyes red-rimmed from crying.

"Jimmy, I want to introduce my sister, Sandy, and our friend, Darcy."

"Hi, Jimmy," Sandy said. "We need to borrow Barney's coat so Darcy's search dogs can track him. Is it in the back seat of your parent's car?"

"You're going to search for Barney?" His brown eyes brightened. "His coat was on the back seat when that car crashed into us. My little puppy got scared and ran away. I'd look for him myself if I didn't have a broken leg." Tears ran down his cheeks. "Find him for me, please?"

"As soon as we leave here, we're going to get Barney's coat and do our best to find him." Darcy smiled. "Try to get some sleep."

After they left the hospital, Darcy obtained police permission and found Barney's coat and rubber toys in the back seat of the Mason's car. She handed them to Sandy. "Put Barney's stuff in that paper bag."

"I'm glad we can get their suitcases too so they'll have a change of clothes and other things they need," Sandy said.

They loaded the Mason's luggage into Sandy's car and dropped it off at the hospital before they drove to the ranch.

Darcy unlocked the kitchen door, and the dogs gave them their usual enthusiastic greeting.

She said, "I'll bring Tiny and my new dachshund, Daisy, in case Barney is hiding in a small place Tiny can't reach." Darcy tied blue bandanas on both dogs so they'd know they were going to work. She explained, "Tiny loves to work. For him it's like play time. Daisy is still in training, learning to fetch, but she loves the biscuit rewards she earns, and she's a fast learner."

Sandy petted the other dogs who looked disappointed they weren't chosen.

Darcy asked Tiny and Daisy, "Do you want to search for a lost puppy?"

Eager to go, they barked and wagged their tails.

She petted her other dogs. "Sorry, guys, but I need you here to guard the house. Sylvester, you're in charge."

The parrot squawked. "Ranch security is on the job."

Darcy put an empty dog crate in her SUV for Barney and tossed his toys inside it. "Okay, let's go." The black and white Great Dane jumped into the back of her SUV, and she set the little brown dachshund down beside him.

It took them about twenty minutes to get to the crash site. Highway Patrol officers had marked the area well, making it easy to find. Darcy parked her vehicle on the side of the road and hooked a thirty-foot reeled lead to the D-ring on Tiny's harness.

"I'll handle Tiny, and you can carry Daisy. Tiny has long legs, but she's too small to go through the thick foliage." She handed the little dachshund to Sandy.

Darcy took Barney's coat out of the paper bag, held it under the dogs' noses, and said, "Take scent."

Then she replaced the coat and ordered Tiny, "Search and find."

FIFTEEN

Tiny splashed through a drainage ditch, and Darcy leaped across it, grateful it wasn't too wide. He searched the water's edge in both directions and picked up Barney's scent in tall grass. They headed north.

Darcy yelled to Sandy, "Tiny found the scent. Better come over here with Daisy and follow us." She waited for Sandy to catch up to her.

Sandy said, "No worries, Daisy isn't heavy. I'll follow you."

A large field bordered a wooded area. Tiny kept his nose to the ground, hot on the puppy's trail. The scent path through the woods led them to a cement slab surrounded by slats of rotted wood decomposing on the ground. Long clay sewer pipes with big oil drums piled behind them completed the site.

"Looks like the remains of an old wooden building," Sandy said.

A loud roar boomed through the woods.

"That's the big cats at Lion Country Safari," Darcy said. "I'll bet poor little Barney never heard anything like that before. He must be terrified."

Tiny led her to one of the narrow sewer pipes. The far end was blocked by a big oil drum. He sat with his paw on the pipe.

Darcy kneeled down and peered inside. She couldn't see anything until she aimed her powerful magnesium flashlight into it. Two small eyes near the back end seemed to glow in her light.

"Good boy, Tiny." She hugged him, moved him away from the opening, reached into her backpack, and handed him a dog biscuit.

She motioned for Sandy to bring Daisy and stood beside the pipe out of the puppy's sight. She put her finger to her lips. "Wait here," Darcy whispered.

She kneeled on the ground. "Here, Barney, come and get a biscuit." She called to him in a soft, coaxing voice, but he was too frightened to come out.

She turned to Sandy. "Give me Daisy." She held the

little dachshund and looked into her eyes. "Daisy, be a good girl and give this biscuit to the puppy in there. Then I'll give you one."

Daisy whined softly to let her know she understood. She held the dog biscuit in her mouth and trotted into the long narrow pipe. Darcy kneeled down and shined her light inside, watching her. Daisy eased up to Barney and set the dog biscuit down in front of him. Then she whined and wagged her tail. Barney remained frozen in place while Daisy backed out, sat up, and begged.

Darcy said, "Good girl, Daisy," and handed her a biscuit. She gobbled it up. Then Darcy gave her another one and said, "Take it to Barney."

She carried it to Barney but dropped it a little farther away and backed out. Daisy sat up and begged for another reward. After she ate her biscuit, she took the next one in and left it farther away than the previous ones.

Daisy lured Barney closer and closer by using a trail of dog biscuits. When she backed out of the pipe, Darcy praised her, gave her a biscuit, and moved her out of sight beside Sandy and Tiny. Then Darcy put a handful of dog biscuits on the ground a few feet in front of the pipe.

In a little while, Barney crawled out dragging his left hind leg behind him.

Poor little hungry dog, injured and afraid. Darcy let him eat the rest of the dog biscuits, then reached behind him and picked him up.

He yipped but calmed down as she gently petted him. His collar ID verified he was the missing dog.

Darcy said, "Jimmy is waiting for you."

His little ears perked up at the sound of Jimmy's name.

She handed him to Sandy and gave Daisy and Tiny more dog biscuits while she praised them for a job well done. She carried Daisy, and Sandy carried Barney as they walked back to her SUV.

Darcy laid Barney on a blanket in the dog crate that held his familiar toys. "You rest now. We're taking you to Jimmy after a quick check up."

After the dogs were loaded into the car, Sandy high-fived Darcy. "Great job!"

She drove them to the animal hospital and told Andy, the veterinarian, Barney's story.

He put the puppy's fractured leg in a cast. "He doesn't have any other injuries. The best medicine for him is to see Jimmy, but he needs a bath before you can sneak him into the hospital. I'll cover the cast with a plastic bag and have my assistant bathe him."

"Thank you, Andy," Darcy said. "Jimmy will be so happy to see Barney."

"Barney will be happy too," Andy said. "Do you think you can sneak him into the hospital?"

Sandy said, "I know exactly how we'll do it. Do you want us to bring them your bill?""

"There will be no charge for my services. It's the least I can do for the family. Keep me informed on how they're doing. I'll help any way I can."

"Thanks again, Andy," Darcy said. "I knew we could count on you."

As they drove back to the ranch, Darcy asked, "How will we smuggle Barney into the hospital?"

"We'll wrap him in a blanket like a baby. I've been sewing baby clothes for my cousin. I have a blue bonnet with a matching dress that would fit him."

"That sounds perfect." Darcy carried Barney into the house, and Daisy, Tiny, and Sandy followed her.

The dogs barked welcomes.

"Hello, Sandy," Sylvester said.

"How are you, Sylvester?"

"It's good to be king." Sylvester bobbed his grey head up and down.

Darcy held Barney as the other dogs followed them

into the kitchen and sat in a row. Darcy gave them each a biscuit and introduced them to Barney.

"Well, don't I get a treat too?" Sylvester asked, indignant. "Don't forget I'm the one who keeps things running smoothly around here when you're not home."

"Sandy, please give him a cracker. They're in the end cabinet. And then let's call Jimmy and tell him we found Barney. I'll put my cellphone on SPEAKER so we can talk to him at the same time."

"Okay, but don't mention our plan to sneak Barney into the hospital in case it doesn't work out. We don't want to disappoint him." Sandy gave Sylvester a cracker and then called Laura at the hospital. She told her they found Barney and asked to talk to Jimmy.

"I can't wait to see Jimmy's face when he hears the good news. I'll take my cellphone to him right now and put it on SPEAKER," Laura said. "Jimmy's mother is conscious now, and the prognosis is good. Hold on, I'm almost there."

Darcy and Sandy heard Laura say, "I have a phone call for you, Jimmy."

Jimmy took the phone and said, "Hello."

"We found Barney," Darcy and Sandy said.

"You found Barney? Is he okay?" Jimmy's voice was

filled with joy.

"Barney has a broken leg, just like you, but he's okay. The vet put a cast on it. You both need to rest and get strong fast so you can be together again," Darcy said.

"I will, I will," Jimmy agreed.

His father shouted a thank you to Darcy and Sandy.

"Thank you, Nurse Laura," Jimmy said as he handed the phone to her.

"I think we should celebrate with ice cream. I'm on my break so I'll get it," Laura said to Jimmy with her phone still on SPEAKER. As she left the room, heading for the cafeteria, she said, "Thanks, girls. I'm glad we could give them good news."

"Switch off the speaker function," Sandy said.

"Okay, it's off. What's the secret?" Laura asked.

"We're going to dress Barney in baby clothes with a bonnet on his head, wrap him in a baby blanket, and sneak him into the hospital. We'll leave in about an hour. Can you gather the family in the mother's private room? We want to close the door so nobody else will see the puppy."

"Sure, I'll look forward to it, but don't let the guards see Barney. I'll meet you at the elevator on the fourth floor."

SIXTEEN

Sandy held sweet-smelling Barney wrapped in a blanket as Darcy drove. He looked so adorable in the blue bonnet they smiled every time they looked at him.

"You're going to see Jimmy," Sandy said.

Barney wagged his tail and licked her face.

"Sandy, you carry him into the hospital because you're tall, and people won't get much of a chance to peek at him. Remember to hold one hand on the blanket by his tail to keep it from wagging." She chuckled. "That would cause a quite a stir if people saw it."

They made it past the security guards and into the elevator without any problems. Sandy stood in the corner, and Darcy stood in front of her until they came to the fourth floor.

When the elevator door opened, Laura was waiting for them. She led them to Mrs. Mason's room four doors down the hallway.

They smiled at Mr. and Mrs. Mason's puzzled expressions. Sandy rocked her bundle back and forth, gently patting the small form under the blanket until Darcy closed the door.

"Jimmy, Sandy has a baby she wants you to hold," Laura said.

"I've never held a baby," Jimmy said as he sat in a wheelchair.

"I'm pretty sure you've held this one. Here you are." Sandy set Barney on Jimmy's lap. His eyes widened when Barney's wagging tail brushed the blanket aside, and he licked Jimmy's face.

"Wha—it's Barney!"

Everyone in the room laughed. "We had to dress him up like a baby to sneak him into the hospital," Sandy said.

Jimmy hugged Barney as his parents smiled.

"Thank you so much!" Jimmy gushed.

"Barney will stay at my house tonight," Darcy said. "Your parents told me they want to recuperate at the hotel where you have reservations for the next three weeks. Call me tomorrow when you're discharged, and I'll drive you to your hotel."

"That's taking too much of your time. We'll get a taxi," Mr. Mason said.

"Honestly, it would be my pleasure," Darcy said.

"You three are angels," Mrs. Mason said, teary eyed.

A little while later, Darcy and Sandy left with Barney.

Light hearted, Darcy looked forward to the next day.

* * *

Later that evening, a television reporter interviewed the family about their accident. Jimmy happily reported the dogs from the Sniffers Agency had found Barney for him, and that Darcy McKay was bringing his dog to the hospital in the morning so she could drive the family to their hotel on Singer Island.

The reporter planned to be at the hospital with a camera crew to film the happy departure.

* * *

The next morning, Darcy drove her Chevy Suburban to the hospital. Barney rode in the back in his crate full of toys. SNIFFERS AGENCY – THE NOSE KNOWS was emblazoned on the sides of her huge white SUV. She'd have plenty of room for the family, Jimmy's wheelchair, and all their luggage.

A small crowd had gathered outside the hospital near the reporter, television van, and camera crew.

Laura walked beside the Mason family's wheelchairs as they were wheeled by orderlies to Darcy's SUV.

The news team filmed Darcy handing Barney to Jimmy. When the little boy's face lit up with joy, all the onlookers cheered.

Jimmy said, "I want to thank Nurse Laura for taking good care of me and my parents. And I also want to thank her sister Sandy, and Darcy, the dog lady, for finding my puppy, Barney. He has a broken leg just like mine."

The reporter asked Darcy for the whole story. She recounted the details and gave credit to Laura, Sandy, and her furry employees.

Then she drove the happy family to their hotel on Singer Island. After ensuring they were settled in a suite, Darcy gave them one of her business cards. "Call me if you need anything. I hope you enjoy the beach."

Darcy's cell rang during the drive back to her ranch. It was Sandy. "I saw the news story. That was good publicity for your business. Maybe you'll get some good-paying jobs now. And thanks for the kind words about me and my sister."

"Hey, it was a team effort. Thanks for helping me with the dogs."

"Oh, don't forget it's your turn to drive to the dance tonight," Sandy said. Laura and I will be ready at eight."

SEVENTEEN

Wanda's White Horse Dance Hall was a favorite night spot for people who lived in Garnet. It was a nice place to socialize with neighbors and make new friends. The band played all kinds of dance music, including country line dances for singles. A huge buffet offered barbequed beef and chicken, potato salad, corn on the cob, sweet-potato fries, potato chips, apple pie, and chocolate cake. The long rectangular-shaped bar served wine, beer, and soft drinks.

The girls wore jeans, western shirts, and boots. Sandy secured a table by the dance floor, while Darcy and Laura went to the bar for a bottle of red wine, three glasses, and bottled waters for the table.

"I'm ready for a fun night of dancing," Darcy said.

Just then, three men they'd known since high school asked them to dance. They enjoyed several dances with them and then took a beverage break.

Resting, Sandy said, "Wow, look at that handsome hunk at the end of the bar. It's hard to see the full view with all those women flocking around him."

Darcy glanced at the bar and back to Sandy. She hesitated a moment and looked again to make sure it really was Scott. He was dressed in a blue western shirt and jeans that emphasized his taut, muscular body. "Oh, no, it's him."

"Him who?" Sandy asked.

"Scott Logan—that new hotshot detective I told you about. He almost arrested me the first time we met. I never expected to see him at a western bar." She turned her head, shielding her face with her hand. "Maybe he didn't see me."

Sandy took another look. "I wouldn't mind getting arrested by *him*." She stared. "He reminds me of someone." She paused, thinking. After another long glance in his direction, she said, "He looks like that handsome movie star who used to play James Bond, but I can't recall his name."

Laura frowned. "Not Sean Connery."

Sandy shook her head. "No, no, I'm thinking of a more recent James Bond."

Darcy heaved a big sigh. "Pierce Brosnan."

"Yes, but younger, of course." Sandy gave her a thumbs up.

Laura asked, "Wasn't he your favorite male movie star in his earlier days, Darcy?"

"Yes, that's why I'm upset. I don't *want* to be attracted to Scott, but I *am*. Men that handsome are never true to one woman. I learned that in college when I had my heart broken. I don't want to go through *that* again."

"Stop staring at him, Sandy," Laura whispered. "He might see you." She smoothed her short brown hair, and a smile crossed her pretty face. "As an experienced nurse who knows the male body inside and out, I'd definitely grade him an A-plus."

Chuck Ryan came up behind Darcy and put his hands on her shoulders. She stiffened, thinking it was Scott.

"Darcy, may I have this dance?" he asked.

She recognized Chuck's voice, breathed a sigh of relief, and smiled. "Yes, I'd love to dance with you."

Chuck whisked her onto the crowded floor for a slow dance. "Scott told me all about his recent experience with you."

She frowned and looked up at him with narrowed eyes. "Exactly what did he tell you?" *If he told Chuck about my blouse disaster, I'll kick him into the next county.*

Puzzled by her tone, Chuck replied, "That your furry employees found the arsonist. He thanked me for recommending your agency, and he praised you, the dogs, and your dad's barbecue dinner." He frowned. "Why? Is something wrong?"

"Oh, I'm sorry. I misunderstood what you said because of the loud music." She smiled and hugged him. "Thanks for the recommendation. I'll make sure you're invited to my dad's next cookout."

"I'll look forward to it. And I'd like to talk to you about a job you and your furry friends can do for me. When can we get together?"

"How about a cookout tomorrow night at the ranch? Will that work for you?"

"Sure." Chuck smiled, his bright brown eyes sparkling with enthusiasm. He ran his hand through his curly brown hair. "Just say the time, and I'll be there. Your dad is famous for his mouth-watering barbecues."

"Why don't you go grab a beer and join us at our table in a few minutes. I'll see if Sandy and Laura want to come tomorrow night." Darcy headed back to her table.

Sandy arrived at the table just as her nemesis, Jennie Martin strolled by with Tom Taylor, Sandy's ex-boyfriend stolen by Jennie.

Jennie smirked at Sandy and said, "Well, look who's here—slutty Sandy."

Sandy stood and got in her face. "Don't ever call me that again. You ruined my reputation in high school with your lies." She looked her up and down. "Better back off the cupcakes at your aunt's bakery. It's starting to show on your hips."

"Is not! In fact, I'm going to New York tomorrow for an interview with the Worldwide Modeling Agency." Jennie struck a pose with her hands on her hips.

Tom turned Jennie around. "What? You promised me you wouldn't go."

"Don't sweat it, sweetheart. Soon you'll have a supermodel on your arm, something slutty Sandy will never be." Jennie tossed her long blond hair, grabbed Tom's hand, and strutted away before Sandy could react to the insult.

Sandy balled her fists. "I hate that lying, phony princess! I hope she chokes on a cupcake and dies."

"Better yet, let's hope she pigs out at the Bodacious

Buns Bakery and ends up weighing three hundred pounds," Darcy said.

Just then, Andy, the local veterinarian, asked Sandy to dance, and she followed him onto the dance floor.

Darcy glanced around and noticed Laura dancing with Scott.

Chuck placed a pitcher of beer on the table with three glasses. "May as well go for another dance until everybody returns to the table." He offered Darcy his hand.

After the dance ended, Chuck pulled out a chair for Darcy and sat beside her. Laura and Scott returned to the table, and Scott asked Sandy for a dance. Then Andy asked Laura, and Chuck danced with Darcy again. They all danced until the band took a break.

After they were all seated back at the table, Darcy said, "I want to invite everyone to a barbecue tomorrow night. My dad is always looking for an excuse to have one. Will you come?"

Everyone smiled and gave her a resounding, "Yes!"

The guys said they'd bring the drinks, and Laura and Sandy agreed to provide desserts.

"May I have this dance?" Scott asked Darcy.

She nodded, and he pulled her chair away from the table, taking charge with quiet assurance. He placed his hand on her lower back and guided her to the dance floor. Then he drew her against him, her soft curves molding to the contours of his lean body as he inhaled her intoxicating scent.

Darcy felt the heat emanating from his body as he bent his head and held her close. He had a vitality and ruggedness that attracted her against her will. Their bodies swayed to the rhythm as they danced in silence while the music flowed from one song to another.

Scott leaned in and gently kissed her neck just beneath her right ear.

His sensual kiss made her tingle inside. Diffusing the situation, Darcy tilted her head back and looked up at him. "It's unusual for a guy as tall as you to be so light on your feet. Did you take dance lessons?"

"No, I gave them." He smiled. "I worked my way through college as a dance instructor." As they walked back to the table, Scott said, "I like your friends."

"They like you too. We'll have a good time tomorrow night."

"Is there anything besides drinks I can bring for the barbecue?"

"Thanks, but no. Dad likes to take care of the rest of it."

Scott monopolized Darcy on the dance floor until closing time when she left with her girlfriends.

On the ride home, Sandy said, "Scott asked me if we were all single. I told him we're definitely available."

"I'm not ready to settle down," Darcy said. "Are either of you?"

Laura and Sandy shook their heads no.

Laura said, "I don't want to get serious with anyone just now, but I really like Andy. He's good looking, fun, and we both work in medicine and love animals."

"I think Scott is interested in you, Darcy," Sandy said. "You were all he talked about when he danced with me. But that's okay. I like Chuck. He's a good dancer, and he has a great sense of humor."

Darcy dropped them off and happily hummed on her way home. When she entered the house, the dogs rushed to greet her.

Sylvester called out, "We're watching TV. Did you have a good time?"

"I had a wonderful time. Dad, everybody was praising your barbecue skills. Let's have another of your famous cookout parties."

"Sure, when?"

"Tomorrow night."

He raised his eyebrows. "That's short notice."

"I invited Sandy, Laura, Chuck, Andy, and Scott. They were at the dance tonight and are bringing drinks and desserts. Do you want to invite anybody else besides your girlfriend, Sally?"

"No, just Sally. Sounds like you have a good group coming. You do the shopping, and I'll do the cooking."

She hugged her dad and the dogs. She even gave Sylvester a cracker before he asked for one.

Sylvester cocked his head to the side and stared at her. "Well, you're in a generous and happy mood. You should go to dances more often."

She smiled. "I'm happy because I had a good time with my friends." She sat at the kitchen table and wrote a shopping list.

Satisfied she had everything planned, she went to bed and slept soundly.

EIGHTEEN

Jennie Martin zipped up her wheeled suitcase and pulled it out to her blue Chevy Volt in the dark parking lot. She tossed the small valise onto the backseat and hung her dress bag on the little hook over the window.

She glanced at her bejeweled watch in the dim, predawn light. *Good, plenty of time to drive to the airport for my eight-a.m. flight.* Jennie folded her five-foot ten, slender body behind the steering wheel and started the engine.

Her boyfriend, Tom, rushed out of her rental apartment, yelling, "Where do you think you're going?"

Jennie gunned the accelerator and peeled out of the parking lot. *The nerve of him, trying to block my modeling career. I'll show him.*

She took the back road along the south side of the lake in case Tom tried to follow her. Her anger and paranoia caused her to pay too much attention to the rearview mirror.

She looked forward too late.

A twelve-foot gator slowly ambled across the road, directly in her path. She swerved to miss the huge reptile and slid into a muddy ditch. Shifting into reverse, she tried to back out, but her little car's front wheels were stuck deep in the soft mud. She couldn't leave her car with the dangerous alligator nearby.

Jennie blew out a sigh and reached into her handbag for her cellphone. She dialed Norman Price of Price Towing Service. This wasn't the first time she'd needed a tow. Norm had pulled her out of a ditch two weeks ago when her little car had hydroplaned during heavy rain. She was glad she had his number in her phone.

Norm's recorded voice came over her cell, "Thank you for calling Price Towing Service. Our regular business hours are 7:00 a.m. to midnight. Please leave a message at the tone."

She glanced at her watch. It was 6:05. She heard the beep and said, "Norm, this is Jennie Martin. My car is stuck in a ditch on Lakeshore Road about five miles southwest of town. Please tow it back to my apartment. I'm going to call an Uber to finish taking me to the airport for my flight to New York. Wish me luck. I've got an interview with Worldwide Modeling Agency today."

Jennie couldn't use the Uber app without an address for pickup, so she called Gary Brown, one of her regular customers at Bodacious Buns Bakery, who she knew was an Uber driver. Gary, in his early forties, was obviously interested in Jennie. He'd flirted with her every morning at the bakery for several months.

"Hello," Gary said, sounding half asleep.

"Gary, it's Jennie. Sorry to call so early, but I'm in serious need of rescue. My car is stuck in a ditch, and I need to catch a flight to New York that leaves in about an hour and a half. Please, will you come and take me to the airport?"

"Where are you, Jennie?"

"About five miles southwest of Garnet on Lakeshore Road. Please, hurry." She looked out the window just as the gator waddled into the brush toward the lake.

"Hang tight. I'll be there in fifteen minutes, but you'll owe me big for this. You have to go out with me when you get back from New York. I'll take you to dinner at Betty's

Bistro and get us a waterfront table."

"Sounds wonderful. Thanks, Gary. I'll see you soon." Jennie frowned as she dropped her phone into her purse. *No way I'll go to dinner with that loser.*

A cream Bentley stopped on the road behind her car, and a tall, handsome, well-dressed man in his mid-thirties got out and walked around to her. He had dark-blue, penetrating eyes and a friendly smile.

"Hello, do you need help?" he asked.

Jennie opened her door, and he offered his hand to help her up the side of the ditch.

"What's a lovely lady like you doing out here so early?" He straightened his French cuffs.

"I was on my way to the airport when I swerved to miss a huge gator." She smoothed her long blond hair.

"So am I." He checked his gold Patek Philippe watch. "I've got a flight to New York at eight o'clock."

Her brown eyes widened. "I'm also on a flight to New York at eight."

"Why don't you ride with me?" He gestured at his car. "You can call a tow truck on the way."

"Thank you. I'll just get my purse and luggage." She turned toward her car.

Before she had a chance to take a step forward, his

gloved hand covered her nose and mouth with a cloth soaked in chloroform while he held her close with his other arm.

Jennie was unconscious in seconds.

When she awoke, she was lying on a single bed in a ten-foot square room without windows, and her left ankle was chained to the bed. She glanced around, feeling confused and dizzy. She focused on a macabre skeleton painting that adorned one wall.

Is this real or am I having a nightmare?

NINETEEN

Alice Martin finished her third cup of coffee at the Bodacious Buns Bakery and glanced at her watch. She carried her cup to the counter where her sister, Millie, stacked brownies on a circular display.

"Jennie should've called me an hour ago," Alice said, frowning. "New York is a dangerous place. What if something happened to her?"

"Have you tried her cell?" Millie asked.

"Of course, but my calls go straight to voice mail." Alice held out her cup for a refill.

"Why don't you switch to a glass of milk and have one of these fresh brownies?" Millie put one on a plate and handed it to her.

"Okay, but skip the milk." Alice took a bite. "Do you think I should check her apartment?"

"Call the airline first. Maybe her flight was delayed." Millie placed a glass dome over the brownie platter.

"Good idea." Alice pulled out a paper with the flight info written on it and tapped in the number. "Hello, I'm checking on my daughter, Jennie Martin. She took your Flight 4230 from Palm Beach International to La Guardia Airport at 8:00 a.m., and I'd like to know if it was delayed." She listened a moment. "It was on time?" She hesitated. "Can you confirm that my daughter was on that flight?" Alice paced while she waited for the answer. "What? Are you sure? Okay, thank you."

"Well? What did they say?" Millie asked.

"Jennie never checked-in for the flight." Alice wolfed down the rest of the brownie.

"Yesterday, Jennie told me that her boyfriend didn't want her to go to that interview," Millie said. "Tom was afraid she'd hit the big time and leave him behind. I hope he didn't do something to stop her."

Alice handed her the empty plate. "I'm going to her apartment."

"Call me as soon as you know something." Millie grabbed a coffee pot and walked around to refill her customers' cups.

Alice drove the four blocks to Jennie's apartment, a cute townhouse in a row of identical apartments. The majority of residents worked during the day, so many of the parking spaces were empty. But not Jennie's spot. Her blue Chevy Volt was in its designated space.

Alice parked beside her daughter's car and walked around to look at it. Mud covered the front wheels, bumper, and part of the hood. The windshield was splattered with mud, which would've made driving difficult.

She pulled out the emergency key Jennie had given her, knocked, and unlocked the front door. "Jennie? Are you home?"

No answer. The apartment was quiet.

She checked every room. When she walked into the bedroom, she headed for the closet where Jennie kept her luggage. The suitcase and dress bag were gone.

Alice got a sick feeling in her stomach and felt a strong intuition that something was terribly wrong. She pulled out her cell and called the Garnet Police Department.

TWENTY

Scott answered the call that had been transferred to his desk. "Detective Logan, how may I help you?"

"Something terrible has happened to my daughter, Jennie. I need you to find her." Alice gave Scott all the details relating to her daughter.

"I'll meet you at her apartment. Expect me in about five minutes." He hung up, grabbed his Glock, and headed out the door.

When he arrived in front of the apartment, he parked behind the Chevy Volt. The car was locked, but he could see a receipt stuck in the center console. He could only read the last part of the name on the paper: Towing Service. A quick Google check on his cell showed one tow company in Garnet: Price Towing Service.

Scott called them.

"This is Norman Price of Price Towing Service. How may I help you?" the friendly man answered.

Scott identified himself and said, "I'm looking into a missing person case. What can you tell me about towing Jennie Martin's car?"

"Jennie's not missing. She got stuck in a ditch early this morning on her way to the airport. She asked me to tow her car home and said she'd take an Uber to the airport—said she had an important interview in New York."

"I need you to show me exactly where you found her car. Meet me at her apartment in thirty minutes." Scott walked to Jennie's apartment and rang the bell.

Alice answered the door. "Detective Logan?"

He flashed his badge. "Have you noticed anything unusual in her apartment?"

"Her bed is unmade. Jennie always tidies the covers and puts on the bedspread, unless . . ."

Scott followed her upstairs to the bedroom. "Unless what?"

"If Tom spent the night, and Jennie left while he was still in bed, or if Tom abducted her to stop her from going to New York." She grabbed his arm. "What if they argued, and he killed her?"

"Is Tom about six feet with sandy blond hair and muscles like a jock?" he asked.

"Yes, how did you know that?" she asked, looking panicky.

"I saw them arguing last night at the dance hall." Scott checked the bed and bathroom for any signs of a struggle. "No blood visible—that's a good sign."

He carefully searched the apartment from top to bottom. Afterward, he paused near the front door. "It doesn't look like anything bad happened here. Let me know immediately if you hear from Jennie." He handed Alice his card.

"Wait, aren't you going to look for her?" Alice fought back tears.

He glanced at his watch. "I'm meeting with the man who towed her car. He's going to show me where she was stuck this morning."

A sharp knock on the door diverted their attention.

Scott opened the door to a short, medium-build man in his mid-thirties.

"Detective Logan? I'm Norm Price. Did you find Jennie?"

"Norm?" Alice pushed past Scott. "What have you done with my Jennie?"

"Nothing, Mrs. Martin. I just towed her car back here like she asked." Norm told them about Jennie's phone call to him early that morning. "By the time I got there, she was gone. She told me she was taking an Uber to the airport."

"Did you see anything personal inside her car—purse, luggage?" Scott asked.

"No, and I didn't expect to see anything since she said she was catching a flight." Norm looked at Scott. "Still want me to show you where I found her car?"

He nodded and glanced at Alice. "Mrs. Martin, go home in case Jennie tries to contact you. I'll call as soon as I know something." He followed Norm to the parking lot.

"Mind if I take my car so I can get back to work if you decide to stay at the site to investigate?" Norm asked.

"That's fine. I'll follow you." Scott climbed into his unmarked police car and started the engine.

On the way, Scott called Chuck. "Jennie Martin is missing. I need you to look around Price Towing Service while Norman Price is busy leading me to where he claims he found her car. Talk to his employees. Ask if they saw her this morning."

"I'll get right on it, Scott. Keep me posted," Chuck said before he hung up.

Ahead, Norm's car slowed, and it was obvious he was looking for something on the lake side of the road. A minute later, he stopped.

Scott parked behind him and got out. "Is this the spot?"

"Yep, see the muddy tracks over there in the ditch. Jennie told me she swerved to miss a big gator." Norm pointed at the tire tracks.

Scott glanced at Norm's muddy boots. "Were you wearing those shoes this morning?"

Norm nodded. "These are my work boots—size nine if that's important."

"It could be very important. Was anyone with you when you towed the car?"

"At zero dark thirty? Nope, just me. Why?" Norm's eyes focused on the area where Scott was looking beside the tire tracks. "Hey, those look like way bigger foot prints."

"They look like size twelve." He held his foot in the air nearby to measure. "You said she called an Uber. These might be the driver's tracks—could be he helped her with her luggage."

"That would be Gary Brown," Norm said. "He's our only Uber driver, but these can't be his footprints. Gary's six-five and three hundred pounds."

"You're right. The prints would be bigger and deeper if he made them." He glanced at Norm. "What makes you think Gary is the only Uber driver in Garnet?"

He shrugged. "Garnet's a small town with lots of rich people who take limos." Norm looked at Scott. "Haven't you wondered why a small community like ours has a bigger than normal police department?"

"I assumed they were expecting a large population growth in the near future and wanted to stay ahead of the curve." Scott used his cell to take pictures of the footprints.

"Nope. The rich people in Banyan Country Estates want lots of cops so they can feel safe. Their taxes paid for your job." Norm glanced around. "Is it okay if I go back to work now?"

"Yes, and thanks for your help." He handed Norm his card. "If you hear from Jennie or learn anything that might help find her, call this number."

After Norm drove away, Scott called the Palm Beach County Sheriff's Department and asked them to send a Crime Scene Unit to gather forensic evidence. "Yes, everything points to abduction or murder. I'm trying to get ahead of this in case there's still a chance we can save her." He listened a moment. "Thank you."

TWENTY-ONE

After dealing with the CSI unit, Scott drove back to the police station to meet with Chuck and see what else they could dig up.

Chuck waved him over to his desk. "Norman Price appears to be clean. Did you find anything where her car was towed?"

"Yeah, at least four different sized men's shoe prints," Scott said. "I called PBSO's CSU team to gather evidence at the tow scene and in the vehicle. So far, our prime suspect is normal weight with a size twelve boot."

"Could be her boyfriend, Tom Taylor," Chuck said. "Remember the fight they had last night?"

"Do you know where he works?" Scott typed some

notes into his tablet.

"Yeah, his dad's company, Taylor Construction. Their offices are on the southern end of town."

"Let's go," Scott said. "I might need backup if his dad gets protective."

Chuck followed him out the door and climbed into the passenger side of his car. "Take Main Street all the way out of town. It's about three miles south."

A few minutes later, he asked, "Is that it?" Scott pointed at a gated complex with big construction vehicles parked on the grounds.

"Yeah, the office is over there." Chuck pointed to the right after they drove through the open gate.

When they entered the office building, a petite blonde behind the reception desk said, "Welcome, gentlemen. How may I assist you?"

They flashed their badges.

"Did Tom Taylor come to work today?" Scott asked.

She sat up straighter. "Is Tom in trouble?"

"No, but he might be an important witness in a case we're working on," Chuck said. "Is he here?"

"He came in this morning on time, like always. Then he checked on the logistics for the project his dad put him in charge of—a big mansion they're building over in

Banyan Country Estates." She punched a button. "Is Tom in his office?"

She glanced at the detectives. "You're in luck. He's meeting with his dad." She stood. "I'll show you to Travis Taylor's office."

They entered an expansive office with display models of office buildings and mansions on pedestal tables.

Two muscular men stood. They both wore clean work boots.

The detectives flashed their badges and introduced themselves.

"Officers, I'm Travis Taylor and this is my son, Tom. Have a seat. How may we help you?" He sat behind his massive desk.

"We'd like to ask Tom a few questions about a case we're working on. He might be an important witness," Scott said, smiling.

"Sure, what do you need?" Tom said.

"We're looking for Jennie Martin. Have you seen her?" Chuck said.

Tom gave a wolfish grin. "I spent the night at her place, but she had to leave early this morning for a flight to New York." He smirked. "She actually thinks she's going to become a famous fashion model. Fat chance."

"Did you see her drive away?" Scott asked.

"Yeah, it was a little before six—still dark outside." His expression changed to one of suspicion. "Why? What's she done?"

"She skidded her car into a muddy ditch, called for a tow, and then disappeared." Chuck looked into Tom's eyes. "Were you still at her apartment when the tow truck arrived with her car?"

"No, I have to be at work at seven, and I like to stop for breakfast first at Debbie's Diner." He looked from one officer to the other. "Did something happen to Jennie?"

Scott pulled out his cell and called the diner. "This is Detective Scott Logan of the Garnet Police. Were you working the breakfast shift today? Uh huh, and did you see Tom Taylor there early this morning? What time? Thank you." He looked at Tom. "I had to verify your alibi—it's protocol. We think someone with size twelve work boots abducted her." He looked at Travis. "Could it be someone who works here and saw Tom with Jennie? Maybe he wanted her for himself."

Tom sat up straighter. "I bet it was that jailbird, Jason Jones. I told you hiring him was a mistake, Dad." He looked at Scott. "Did her car get stuck along South Lakeshore Road going westbound?"

"Why do you ask?" Chuck said.

"Because Jason lives in a little trailer in the woods just off that road, and he takes that route east to work early every morning. He would've seen her in the ditch."

"Where is he right now, and where exactly does he live?" Scott asked, ready to tap it into his tablet.

Travis picked up his phone. "Let me check and make sure he's there before I send you to the construction site." He talked to his foreman and his tone became tense. "What time? Thanks." He looked at Scott and Chuck. "Jason told the foreman he wasn't feeling well and left about an hour ago. He lives at 27 South Lakeshore Road."

"Thank you. We'll check him out." Scott stood, and Chuck followed him out the door.

They rushed to the address and spotted a car parked next to the trailer.

Scott turned to Chuck. "I'll go to the front door while you check and see if there's another exit."

Scott knocked on the door and heard movement inside. "Police, open up!"

"I'm sick. Go away," a male voice said.

"Open the door now or I'll break it down!" Scott shouted, his Glock in his right hand.

Chuck joined him. "No other way out," he whispered.

He drew his gun.

The door clicked open a crack, and Scott yanked it open. "Hands on your head! Do it now." He shoved the tall, wiry young man backward, spun him around, and cuffed his hands behind his back.

Jennie Martin's purse, suitcase, and clothes bag were open and in plain view.

Scott pinned Jason against the wall. "Where is she?"

"Where's who?" the frightened man asked.

"The woman you kidnapped, Jennie Martin." Scott pointed at the stolen items. "Those are her belongings."

"Wait, you've got this all wrong. I found that stuff in an abandoned car—that makes it finders' keepers. I never saw no girl."

Chuck said, "Look, you've already got a record. This'll go a lot easier for you if you tell us where she is. Don't make this worse than it has to be."

Scott pulled out his cell and called the PBSO CSI unit. "We found Jennie Martin's purse and luggage in a trailer at 27 South Lakeshore Road. The suspect is refusing to tell us what he did with her." He glanced at his watch. "Thanks. We'll wait for you outside."

Scott and Chuck tried in vain to get information about Jennie from Jason while they waited for the forensics team to arrive. Once the CSU people were on site, they took Jason to their lockup at the Garnet Police Department and met with Chief McKay.

TWENTY-TWO

A Windowless Room

Jennie slept fitfully and woke when a short, ugly man with big muscles and stringy hair delivered a tray with iced tea and a club sandwich for her lunch. He left before she had a chance to talk to him.

She got up and sat at the table beside the weird painting. The food smelled good, and she was hungry, so she ate it.

Eventually, the afternoon ended, according to her watch. About an hour before dinner time, the door opened, and a tall, well-dressed man walked in wearing a skeleton mask. She recognized his ruby cuff links.

"Why are you wearing that mask? I already know what you look like."

He pulled out a chair and sat beside her bed. "What makes you think that?"

"I remember you from this morning—tall, good-looking, well-dressed, and those beautiful ruby cuff links." She paused. "And I recognize your voice too."

He shrugged. "Very well." He pulled off the mask and put it on the table.

"Much better. I don't know why you'd want to cover such a handsome face."

"Do you like to play games?" he asked.

"Oh, baby, we could play some *fun* games." She smoothed her blond hair. "And you don't need to chain me to the bed. I find you very attractive—much more than my loser ex-boyfriend. I'll make you feel real good."

"Can you play chess?"

"No."

"Backgammon?"

"No."

"Checkers?"

"No."

"Do you know *any* games?"

Jennie grinned. "I can play strip poker."

"Strip poker, huh. What are the rules?"

"We each have a glass filled with our favorite alcoholic beverage. Whoever loses the hand, drains their glass and removes an item of clothing. The glass is refilled, and we play another hand. Each time someone loses a hand, they remove another item of clothing and empty their glass. By the end of the game, one of us will be drunk and naked. Want to play?"

He smiled. "All right. What's your favorite drink?"

"Rum and coke, preferably Bacardi." She smiled and batted her lashes.

"I'll be back in a few minutes." He stood and left the room.

Jennie found a brush in the bathroom and fixed her hair. She straightened her dress and checked her reflection in the mirror. Not bad, considering. She repaired some smudges of mascara under her eyes.

She returned to the bedroom seconds before her abductor returned. He carried a tray with an ice bucket, Bacardi bottle, liter of cola, bottle of merlot, and two glasses.

He placed the tray on one side of the table. "Ready to play?"

"You know it, handsome." She stroked his arm and sat

across from him.

"Would you like to mix your drink so you get it the way you like it?" he asked as he poured a glass of red wine for himself.

She filled her glass with ice, poured in a generous portion of rum, and topped it off with cola. "I'm ready to play. Would you like me to deal?"

"Be my guest." He handed her a deck of cards.

Jennie dealt the cards and grinned when she looked at hers. Her opponent kept a poker face.

As the hand progressed, he said, "Your blond hair is quite lovely."

"Thank you—I'm a natural blonde." She twirled her long hair around her fingers.

He stared at her and said, "I call."

She grinned and showed her hand. "A pair of kings."

He spread his cards face up. "Four aces."

"Ooh, you win." She stood and pulled off her dress, exposing her bra, panties, garter belt, and stockings. She did a flirtatious twirl and then sat down and chugged her drink.

He leaned back with a satisfied grin. "Excellent."

A look of alarm clouded her face, followed by a sharp intake of breath. Her mouth and nose foamed with liquid as her lips turned blue.

Her wide brown eyes stared straight ahead, unseeing.

* * *

He sipped his wine, savoring the moment. "What a stupid girl you were," he said to the corpse. "You weren't even a good poker player. No reason to keep you around. It'll be fun watching the police find you and fail to catch me."

The short man entered the room and asked, "Bury her like the others?"

"No. Help me put her dress back on. Then we'll put her in the back of your pickup, cover her with a tarp, and you'll dump her body in the lake. Find a secluded spot along the western shoreline in the wildlife refuge and wade her out into deep water so she'll wash up on the town side sometime tomorrow after the strong west wind pushes her. Wear gloves and be careful not to leave any evidence."

TWENTY-THREE

Later that evening, Scott and Chuck arrived at the McKay ranch together, and Laura and Sandy arrived ten minutes later. Then Sally drove up with Andy's car close behind her.

The dogs welcomed everyone by sniffing them and wagging their tails in recognition.

"I'm warning everyone to keep an eye on our famous guzzler, Tiny. Don't let him steal your drinks," Joe said.

Scott looked at the girls. "I guess everyone heard about Jenny Martin going missing. We think we caught the guy who took her, but we haven't found her yet."

Joe shook his head. "It's not looking good for her, but we may find her alive after all."

Sandy said, "I saw her last night at the dance. She was her usual nasty self."

"Yeah, I remember you two had a brief argument," Andy said.

"It's hard to feel bad for someone like her," Sandy said. "She spread lies about me and ruined my reputation in high school."

Laura joined in. "And then she stole Sandy's boyfriend."

Scott stared at Sandy. "Where were you early this morning?"

"Am I a suspect?" she asked.

"No, but it would look good in my report if I could account for everyone who had a beef with her." He looked at Sandy. "Well?"

"I went into Dye to be Beautiful at six this morning and logged into their computer to finish my beauty article for the *Garnet Gazette* before I had to start my work day at the salon. I emailed the article to the newspaper when I finished it at six-thirty. Then I walked over to Bodacious Buns Bakery for coffee and a hot croissant, and returned to the beauty parlor by seven to prepare for my clients."

"Good, that'll be easy to check." Scott made notes on his tablet.

Darcy frowned at him. "Really, Scott?"

"This way nobody can say we didn't look into every possibility, no matter how remote, and Sandy can say we cleared her if anybody tries to give her a hard time." He put his tablet back into his jacket pocket.

"Okay, grab your drinks and carry them outside." Darcy led the guests to the party area by the grill.

As they sat around the large picnic table, Chuck said, "Darcy, I have a problem I'm hoping you can help me solve."

"What is it?"

"I received a call from a lady living in one of the little neighborhoods just outside town. She suspects her next-door neighbors are selling drugs from their home, probably opioids. Do you have a drug-sniffing dog that could verify it?"

"Are you saying you have a search warrant and want the house searched for drugs?" Darcy asked.

"No, I need more than a neighbor's word to get a warrant. Would one of your dogs be able to pick up a drug scent on whoever answers the door?"

Darcy nodded. "Dobie can do it if the person has been in contact with the drugs or has some on them, and I have the perfect cover. The Humane Society is selling raffle tickets for a cruise to the Bahamas. I planned on going door-to-door, representing the local branch, with Dobie wearing his Humane Society bandana. Give me the address, and I'll stop at the suspect's house, along with every house in the surrounding six-block area."

"How will you know if the dog smells drugs?" Chuck asked.

"Dobie will place his paw on the suspect's leg. The law refers to that as a scent lineup, and it's admissible in court. I'll take a photo with my cellphone, documenting it for you."

"I can go with you and work the other side of each street," Sandy offered, always eager to help.

"That would be great," Darcy said. "We work well together. I'll let you take Laddie. He's always a crowd pleaser."

"Sounds like a good plan." Chuck grinned. "When can you do it?"

"Most people are home on weekends," Darcy said. "Would tomorrow be convenient for you, Sandy?"

"Sure, what time?"

"If we leave at nine, we should get to the area by nine-thirty and be finished by lunch time."

Sandy nodded. "I'll be at your house a few minutes

before nine."

Chuck took a map out of his car and spread it on the table. He circled the house he wanted them to check for drugs. "Here it is: 121 Crooked Palms Street."

The chief announced, "The barbequed ribs are ready."

Darcy folded the map, took it into the house, and returned with the potato salad. Sandy, Laura, and Sally carried the rest of the side dishes and desserts to the table.

The guys were deep into crime stories when the ladies sat down. After everyone ate their fill of the chief's barbequed ribs, desserts were served. The men were careful to try a little of each dessert and make a big fuss to please all the women.

Then the table was cleared, and everyone heaped praise upon the host and hostess. The dogs were given the meat scraps, and the rest of the evening was spent with everyone engaging in lively conversation. It was eleven-thirty before all the guests went home.

"Well, Dad, you can chalk up another winner." Darcy patted his back. "You're a great chef."

He smiled, a twinkle in his brown eyes. "You're just saying that because it's true." He gave her a playful pat on her backside.

She smiled and punched his arm. "What a braggart!

You sound just like Sylvester."

"I'll take that as a compliment," Sylvester squawked and fluttered his wings.

TWENTY-FOUR

At nine o'clock Saturday morning, Darcy drove Dobie, her Doberman Pinscher, Laddie, her yellow Labrador retriever, and Sandy to the suspects' neighborhood.

The dogs wiggled and whined, eager to get started. She and Sandy wore Humane Society badges and carried backpacks loaded with dog biscuits, bottled water, and plastic bowls for the dogs. Cellphones, pencils, note-pads, and raffle tickets filled their cargo pockets. The dogs wore their yellow Humane Society bandanas as they proudly pranced from house to house.

Darcy worked one side of the street, and Sandy took the other side, one block at a time. Residents loved the dogs and fawned over them. The dogs enjoyed the attention and were the best advertisement for the Humane Society.

Parents took photos of the dogs with their children, and everyone bought raffle tickets for the cruise. After working the five nearby streets, they ended on the suspects' block.

Darcy met Sandy in the middle of the street. "This is working out great. I've sold tickets to every house so far."

"I did too. This was a great idea. It's because of Laddie my tickets are selling so fast. People fuss over him, and he loves it."

Darcy smiled. "If I sell two tickets to each houscholder on my side of this street, I'll have sold my entire supply."

"I'm almost out of tickets too. When we finish, let's go to the park we passed on the way here and eat our lunch."

"That's a great idea," Darcy said, as she turned and walked toward the potential drug house. She held a drug sample supplied by the Garnet P.D. under his nose and instructed Dobie to identify the drug dealer.

She pocketed the pills and rang the doorbell. Her dog stood beside her in rapt attention, his nose ready for action.

An attractive, dark-haired woman opened the door.

Darcy said, "Hi, I'm selling raffle tickets for a cruise to

the Bahamas for the benefit of the Humane Society. They're only two dollars each. How many would you like?"

"I'll buy two. My, you sure do have a big dog. Is he friendly?"

"Oh, yes, he's very friendly, and he likes to shake hands."

Dobie wagged his stub tail and gently sniffed the woman.

"Is that why he's putting his paw on my leg? He wants to shake my hand?"

"Yes, do you mind?"

"No problem, he's adorable."

"May I take a photo of you together?"

"Wait a minute." The woman swept her hair behind her shoulders, tilted her head back, and twisted into a pose that accentuated her curves. She smiled. "Okay, take the photo."

Dobie put his paw on the woman's leg as Darcy snapped the photo.

Bingo! You've just been tagged as a drug dealer, and that identification will stand up in court.

"Good boy, Dobie!" Darcy gave him a dog biscuit, petted him, and walked to the next house.

She sold the rest of her tickets to the remaining houses

on the street before she met Sandy at the end of the block. "The woman at 121 Crooked Palms has the scent of drugs on her. I got her picture with Dobie."

She and Sandy high-fived.

Sandy glanced at her watch. "I'm surprised we finished before one o'clock. Now we can go and have lunch."

When they arrived at the park, they watered and fed the dogs and then sat on a bench and ate their sandwiches.

"I feel good about this morning," Darcy said. "We completed the job before it got too hot, and we accomplished everything we set out to do. I wonder how the other Humane Society members are doing with their ticket sales."

"I don't know. Of course, Bert and Betty Hancock always outsell everyone because they're well liked, and they belong to a lot of organizations." Sandy took a sip of cola. "I dropped off some tickets at local pet shops, and they agreed to help sell them."

"That was a great idea." Darcy's cellphone rang. Her caller ID indicated it was Chuck. "Hi, Chuck, mission accomplished. Dobie identified the woman drug dealer, and I have a photo proving it. Plus, we sold all our raffle tickets in the process."

"Great, it was a win, win situation," Chuck said.

"It sure was," Darcy said. "We just finished eating our lunch, and now we're going to let the dogs enjoy the park for a while."

"I should have called earlier, but we were busy. Scott and I planned to take you hard-working girls to a late lunch, but you finished sooner than we expected."

"We appreciate the thought. Maybe another time. I'll write a report for you with a copy of the photo. Do you want me to bring it in or email it?"

"You and Sandy can have dinner with Scott and me tonight, and give it to me then. The four of us can go to a movie afterward. What do you say?"

"That's fine with me. I'll give the phone to Sandy, and you can ask her," Darcy said, putting her phone on speaker.

Sandy listened to Chuck's suggestion and said, "Sounds good to me. What time?"

"How about six o'clock? We'll pick you both up in my car. Thanks for a great job," Chuck said. "I'll see you tonight."

TWENTY-FIVE

"Well, shoot!" Scott said, when Chuck told him the women had already eaten lunch.

"The good news is they agreed to dinner and a movie with us tonight." Chuck grinned.

"Well played, my friend." Scott patted Chuck's back. "Let's grab a burger at Betty's Bistro. Some fresh lake air will do us good, and the lunch crowd has probably thinned out enough for us to score a lakeside table."

The detectives parked near the restaurant on Lakeshore Drive and strode through the charming dining room to the popular tables on the outdoor terrace.

"We'd like that empty waterfront table." Scott smiled at the waitress and pointed.

It was a warm, sunny day with a steady wind blowing

across the lake from the western shore, which was bordered by the nature preserve.

Chuck took in a deep breath. "I love the scent of lake water mixed with an occasional whiff of marine fuel."

Scott nodded. "Makes me want to go fishing."

A woman at the next table said, "Hello, Officer Ryan. Molly and I would like to pick up the lunch tab for you and your colleague."

Chuck smiled and nodded. "That's kind of you and your sister, Mrs. Calder."

"Best call me, *Miss* Calder. I'm a widow these past few years, and so is my twin."

"Right, *Miss* Calder." He hesitated. "Would you lovely ladies care to join us?"

"Thank you, dear, but no. We're almost finished," Mary said.

"We like to help out law enforcement whenever we can," Molly said. "Y'all do such a good job keeping us safe."

Scott half-turned and waved a thank you. When he turned back, he whispered, "You know those older ladies?"

"Everyone in Garnet knows the twins." Chuck glanced at the menu. "Mary and Molly Calder started an elite community on the north side of the lake called Banyan Country Estates. One billionaire and lots of multi-millionaires live there."

A waitress stopped at their table, order pad at the ready. "What'll it be?"

"I'd like the Angus beef burger, medium, with sweet-potato fries and iced tea," Scott said.

"Make that two." Chuck gave the young waitress a big smile. When she walked away, he said, "I'm planning to bust that drug house right after lunch. Care to join me?"

"If you've got enough men for backup, I should stay on the Jennie Martin case. It's been over thirty hours since she went missing." He shrugged. "I'm still hoping we find her alive.

Two high-pitched screams shattered the mid-afternoon serenity of the lakefront.

Mary and Molly Calder jumped up. Molly poked Scott in the back.

He stood and turned. "What—"

Wide eyed, she pointed at something floating in the lake, bumping against the concrete seawall.

Scott looked down at the water. A bloated young woman with blond hair stared up at him. "Oh no, it's Jennie Martin."

TWENTY-SIX

Darcy and Sandy watched the dogs play in the park for a while and then loaded them in the car and headed for home. On the way, the air conditioner in the SUV made a clanking noise and stopped working.

Darcy opened the windows. "I need to stop at the Carriage House Garage and see if Bob can fix it. Do you mind?"

"You can't drive in South Florida without air conditioning," Sandy said.

They parked outside Bob's garage, and he inspected the car's air-conditioning system. "I need to order a part. You'll have to leave your car here. I'll work on it first thing Monday morning."

"We'll have to take the dogs home first and then come back. How will I get home after I leave it here?"

"I'll follow you and drive you home in my car," Sandy offered.

"Thanks, Sandy." Darcy turned to Bob. "We'll be back as soon as we drop the dogs off."

Darcy took her car to Bob's, and Sandy drove her home. Darcy was quiet, worrying about the repair bill.

"What's the matter?" Sandy asked.

"I'm worried about the cost. I'm barely able to pay my bills as it is. My dad co-signed the bank loan to get my business started, and I promised I'd make a profit within two years or close my business and apply to the Police Academy. I haven't made a profit yet, and the deadline is getting closer."

Sandy frowned. "I know your dad wants you to be a cop like him." She paused. "If you hadn't worked for free all those times, like you did for Billy's parents when you found Barney, you would've made a profit by now." She sighed. "Of course, I'm not one who should give you advice about money. I mean, look at me—I'm like you. I give away more of my beauty products than I sell."

"I'll put the repairs on my credit card and hope for the best. If I join the police force, maybe there's a way that I can still do my search-and-rescue work part time."

They were quiet the rest of the drive as Darcy thought about her future.

"Let me know if I can help you, other than financially." Sandy leaned over and hugged Darcy.

"Just being able to talk to you about it helps a lot. Thanks, Sandy."

When Darcy entered her house, she asked, "How were things on the home front while I was gone, Sylvester?"

"Tiny, Max, and Daisy were disappointed you didn't take them with you today. You'd better smooth things over by giving them treats, and I could use some too."

Darcy passed out treats for everyone and tried to stop worrying about her company's future.

Her cell rang, and the caller ID indicated her dad was calling. "Hi, Dad, what's up?"

"Where are you right now?" he asked, his tone serious.

"I'm home with Sylvester and the fur babies. What's wrong?"

"You'd better sit down, sweetheart." He hesitated. "Maybe pour yourself a glass of milk and have some of those chocolate-chip cookies left over from last night."

She sucked in a deep breath. "All this stalling is scaring me—out with it."

"Scott and Chuck found Jennie Martin's body floating in the lake by Betty's Bistro this afternoon." He sighed. "Sorry, honey."

"Do they know the cause of death?" she asked, her mind racing.

"Nothing obvious—we'll have to wait for the autopsy results. I might run a little late. Will you be home tonight?"

"Sandy and I are having dinner with Chuck and Scott, and then we're going to a movie."

"Good. It'll take your mind off the bad news. Try to have some fun tonight."

TWENTY-SEVEN

Chuck picked up Sandy and then Scott. Their last stop was the McKay ranch.

Scott rang the bell on the kitchen door, and Sylvester squawked, "Darcy, Scott is here."

Darcy plugged in the electric coffee pot on the counter next to Sylvester's TV and programmed it so all she'd need to do when she came home was press the start button. The dining room table was set for four, and her pecan pie was in a covered dish on the table ready to serve.

"Sylvester is in charge until I come home. Guard the house, Ranch Security Team." She opened the door. "Hello, Scott, and thanks for inviting me."

He smiled. "You look lovely, as always."

"Thank you. You look nice, too."

Scott held the car door open for her and then joined her in the back seat.

Chuck said, "How about Ruby's for dinner?"

"That's a good choice. Darcy and I like their salad bar, and they have a good menu," Sandy replied.

Nervous, Scott tapped his knees with his hands as he listened to the music on the car radio. He turned to Darcy. "Any idea which movie you'd like to see after dinner?"

"There's a new action movie Sandy and I planned to watch later this week. Want to see it tonight?"

Scott nodded. "That's our kind of movie, isn't it, Chuck?"

"Yep, and we need a good distraction after finding Jennie this afternoon."

"That must've been rough," Sandy said.

He glanced back at Scott. "Molly Calder fainted, and Scott caught her a split second before she would've fallen into the lake."

Scott nodded. "Yeah, she probably would've landed on top of the body."

"Whoa, good thing you caught her." Darcy patted his knee. "Jennie's disappearance and murder has been a total nightmare. I hope you catch the killer soon."

Chuck parked near the restaurant on Lakefront Drive,

and the couples strolled down the sidewalk, taking in the mild evening air on their way to dinner.

During the meal, everyone avoided mentioning Jennie. After the couples finished a delicious dinner, they chatted awhile before going to the movie.

Scott asked Darcy, "I didn't see your dad's car in the driveway. Does he have a date tonight?"

"No, he has to work late," she said. "The mayor wants him to speak tonight at an evening press conference about Jennie's murder. Then he has to deal with lots of paperwork about the case."

Chuck asked, "Do they have the cause of death, Scott?"

Scott's phone dinged, and he looked at the message. "The chief just texted me that the medical examiner rushed some tests for toxins and discovered Jennie had been poisoned with cyanide. He said that means the guy in custody probably isn't the killer, and to tell Darcy he'll be there late looking into potential suspects."

"Wait, are you saying the killer is still out there?" Sandy asked.

Scott frowned. "And when we drop her off later, Darcy will be all alone way out there in the country. Not good."

Darcy arched her eyebrows. "*Seriously?*"

"Oh, right." Scott chuckled. "I forgot about your dogs."

TWENTY-EIGHT

Ralph, a strung-out, disheveled young man, slowly drove down the country roads, looking for a dark house with no cars in the driveway. He desperately needed money to buy drugs. If he couldn't find cash, he planned to steal anything of value and pawn it.

"Finally," he muttered as he rubbed the stubble on his jaw. "A dark, isolated farmhouse with no vehicles in the driveway and only one outdoor light on the barn." He noticed a forest bordered the dead-end road. "Even better."

I'll park behind the barn so no one will see my car from the road.

After he parked the car, he walked around the home's

perimeter, looking for a posted sign, warning the house was protected by a home security system. He didn't see one.

Meanwhile, Darcy's alert, four-footed ranch security team had heard the car and picked up the scent of the intruder as he walked around the outside of the house. Max silently went to the kitchen to inform Sylvester, who was in charge. Max's team followed him and listened as he softly whined to Sylvester, alerting him that someone was outside.

Sylvester mimicked Joe's voice in a whisper, "I heard his car coming up the driveway, so I turned off my TV. You guys stay out of sight and don't make a sound when he breaks into the house. It's boring when our humans aren't here. I want to have some fun before I give you the command to take down the intruder."

Max and Dobie hid in the kitchen pantry behind a partially-opened door, Laddie crawled under the large dining room table, Tiny crouched behind a living-room sofa, and Daisy hid under a chair at the kitchen table.

Ralph frowned as he checked the locks on both the front and back steel doors, which only had peep holes. Then he shined his flashlight into each bedroom window.

All the beds were empty. He took off the screen on a

rear bedroom window, leaned it against the house, and tapped a rock against the glass above the window lock. He reached in, unlocked it, opened the window, and crawled inside. Shining his flashlight, he looked around the dark room.

Good, a man's bedroom with a lot of shooting trophies. That means he has guns. I can always sell those fast.

Ralph slowly crept into the den.

Crap! He has a combination lock on his gun safe.

Frustrated, he looked around the room for anything worth stealing. After going through all the desk drawers and finding nothing of value, he took the laptop computer, printer, and calculator. He set them on a wheeled desk chair and pushed the chair into another bedroom, looking for more things he could sell. He took a jewelry box, then rummaged through dresser drawers and closets.

Sylvester tired of waiting for the burglar to come into the kitchen. The outdoor barn light shining through the window and the stove light enabled him to see around the kitchen, especially with his keen bird vision.

He hopped from his perch beside the counter to the electric coffeemaker and used his beak to push the glowing red button. When it switched on, he hopped back to his perch to wait for the burglar.

Ralph stiffened when he heard an odd sound. He stood still for a few minutes, trying to identify it. In moments, the aroma of coffee wafted down the hallway, and he realized the noise was from a percolating coffeemaker. He turned off his flashlight, pulled out his pocketknife, and slid his back along the hallway wall as he crept toward the kitchen to investigate. Squinting in the dim light, he couldn't see anyone, so he assumed the coffeemaker was on a timer. That meant the owners would be home soon, but before he left, he wanted to see if they had any beer. Ralph turned on his flashlight and pointed it at the refrigerator.

A man's voice shouted, "Freeze! Put your hands up and turn around slowly."

Ralph almost wet his pants. *This guy must be a weirdo, hiding in the dark house all this time and watching me.*

He trembled and slowly turned. The flashlight in his raised hand pointed to the ceiling, casting a soft light in the kitchen. He didn't see anyone. "Where ... where ... are you?"

"It doesn't matter where I am. Put your weapons on the floor!"

"I … I … only have a pocketknife and a flashlight."

"Lay them on the floor in front of you—now!"

"Okay, okay, I'm putting them on the floor." Ralph lowered his arms to put the items down, and as he did, his flashlight shined on a grey parrot.

The parrot squawked, "Get that light out of my eyes, dimwit!"

Ralph recognized the voice. "You're not a man. You're a parrot."

"I'm surprised an idiot like you can recognize the difference. I'm Sylvester, head of ranch security. Put your hands behind your head and sit on the floor right now, or you'll be sorry."

"I'm not stupid. If this ranch was protected by a security system, there would be a sign outside."

"A dummy like you belongs in the Dimwit's Protection Program. Our security team operates undercover."

"I don't believe anything you say. You're just a stupid parrot." He picked up his flashlight and pocketknife. "You can't do anything to me, but I can wring your neck." He took a step forward but stopped when he heard growling.

"Take him down guys!" Sylvester shouted.

Ralph heard movement coming from the hallway and to the right and left of him. He shined his flashlight around the room and saw several pairs of blazing yellow eyes as they slowly surrounded him. He trembled at the sight of the large snarling dogs.

He spun around, trying to get away from the dogs, yelling, "Stop! Stop! I won't hurt the parrot. Please, don't bite me!" His flashlight and pocketknife flew across the room when Max leaped on Ralph's back, knocking him down face-first on the tile floor.

"Aw geez, did you hear a crunch? I think Mr. Dimwit broke his nose. Don't let him move a muscle," Sylvester ordered.

Tiny sat on the unconscious burglar's back, Laddie sprawled across his legs, Dobie sat on his right arm, and Daisy squatted on his left arm. Max sat on the floor with his big paw on the man's head while they waited for Darcy.

"Good work, Ranch Security." Sylvester proudly puffed up his feathers. "Guard the perp until Darcy or the chief comes home."

TWENTY-NINE

A few minutes later, Chuck pulled into the McKay driveway, and Darcy unlocked the kitchen door. She flipped on the light and gaped at the unexpected sight on the floor.

Sylvester shouted, "Surprise!"

"What happened?" Darcy asked as she and her friends stood in shocked amazement.

The dogs proudly wagged their tails and looked at Darcy while Sylvester puffed out his feathers. "Let me tell you how *I* captured this stupid perp."

The dogs turned and growled at Sylvester.

"Excuse me," Sylvester said. "I meant to say *we*."

The dogs faced Darcy again and wagged their tails.

Scott and Chuck burst out laughing, and Sandy grabbed her smartphone and snapped a picture. "I've got to show this to Laura."

Scott, Chuck, and Darcy took pictures with their phones too.

"This is how it went down," Sylvester said, mimicking Joe's voice. "I had my security team hide until I gave the order to take him." He focused on Scott. "Book 'em, Dano!"

Scott laughed, and Chuck pulled out his handcuffs.

"I think Sylvester watches too many episodes of Hawaii Five-O," Chuck said.

The girls applauded.

"We appreciate the applause, but we'd prefer treats," Sylvester said.

Darcy praised Sylvester and the dogs and petted all of them.

Scott said, "I'll call for a patrol car and paramedics, then Chuck and I will check the rest of your house. I don't think this guy walked here. He might have an accomplice waiting in a car hidden somewhere close by."

Chuck kneeled down, handcuffed the moaning burglar, and turned him over. "I recognize this guy. I've arrested him for drugs more than once."

Groggy, the burglar mumbled, "Don't let the dogs get me."

Sylvester flapped his wings for attention. "Somebody, pass the treats."

Ignoring the guy on the floor, Darcy pulled out the biscuit and cracker boxes and handed out the treats.

"Chuck and I'll search outside while the dogs guard the perp." Scott glanced at the prisoner, who seemed terrified of the dogs.

The big dogs bared their teeth for effect, and Daisy snarled.

Darcy said, "Guys, take Dobie and Laddie with you. They'll lead you to his car."

Laddie and Dobie rushed to the door to accompany the men. As soon as they were outside, both dogs sniffed the ground and ran behind the barn to the parked car. The keys were in it.

"These dogs could teach our K-9 units a thing or two." Chuck grinned.

They checked the car for stolen items and didn't find any. As they walked back to the house, paramedics and several patrol cars roared into the driveway.

Officer Murphy rushed to meet them. "Is Darcy okay? The chief will be furious when he hears about this."

"Everyone is fine, except the burglar," Scott said.

"That's a relief, especially after what happened to Jennie Martin," Murphy said.

The paramedics took care of the thief, who was anxious to get away from the dogs.

"We have something to show you," Chuck said. He and Scott pulled out their cellphones and showed Murphy, the other officers, and the paramedics the photos of how the dogs had secured the perp.

The men howled with laughter as they looked at the pictures and listened to their story.

After the first responders left, Darcy gave each dog a large biscuit and Sylvester an extra treat before she and her friends enjoyed their dessert.

"Darcy, you should enlarge a copy of your dogs' photo and have it framed to hang on the wall," Sandy said.

"That's a great idea," she said, taking a sip of coffee.

After dessert, Chuck said, "It's getting late. We'd better get going."

As Darcy walked them to the door, Sandy gave her a hug and said, "Laura is going to love this photo. Thanks for a fun evening. It was a welcome distraction after what happened to Jennie. Let me know if you need a ride to get your car."

"Thanks for the dessert and evening entertainment," Chuck said as he gave her a friendly hug. "It really helped to have a brief break from Jennie's case."

Scott said, "Yes, it did. Let's do this again soon. Darcy, if you need to go someplace before your dad gets home, let me know, and I'll take you." Scott smiled, gave her a quick hug, and followed Chuck and Sandy to the car.

When her dad arrived home later, Darcy showed him the photos of the dogs and the burglar, while Sylvester proudly related every detail about the security team's triumph.

Joe laughed so hard tears ran down his cheeks. "This is a nice break from dealing with Jennie's murder, and it proves what I already knew. I never have to worry about leaving you alone. I've got a big op tomorrow, but I can drive you to get your SUV on my way to work if we leave early. Do you have enough money to pay the repair bill? "

"I can manage if it's not too expensive," Darcy said. "I'll put it on my credit card."

Darcy went to bed thinking she couldn't have better protection at home.

THIRTY

When Chief McKay arrived at the police station early the next morning, Chuck and Scott were already there, along with men from the department of Alcohol, Tobacco, Firearm's, and Explosives. He shook hands with them and asked, "Ready for the raid?"

The lead fed adjusted his Kevlar vest and nodded. "A SWAT team from the Sherriff's office is en route to meet us at the target house."

The chief pulled on a vest. "What else do you need?"

"Your mobile communications unit and the personnel to operate it. We borrowed FPL trucks, and our men are disguised as uniformed employees. We have men ready to block off the street and evacuate the houses near the target. They'll explain there's a gas leak. Can you spare enough men to handle the operation?"

"We've got a murder to investigate, but that can wait a few hours. This raid took weeks to plan."

The ATFE officer smiled. "Good. You'll direct the raid from the mobile unit. The utilities trucks will move into position after nine this morning. That'll give the people in the houses time to leave for work or school before we block entry."

Chief McKay assigned Sergeant Collins to be in charge of the police station in his absence and Officer Murphy to drive them in the mobile unit.

* * *

Meanwhile, back at the McKay ranch, Darcy had just driven home in her repaired SUV when her cellphone rang.

She answered it and listened to a report about an abused dog. "Yes, I'll check on the dog. Thanks for calling."

Darcy drove to the neighborhood and was dismayed to find the street blocked off. She circled the block, counted the houses, and parked on the street behind the house she wanted to investigate.

Carrying a shoulder bag full of dog treats and bottled water, she walked through a vacant home's yard that had a for-sale sign posted near the mailbox. She peered through a chain-link fence at the dog abuser's house. A skeletal pit bull was chained to a pole without any shade or water. She climbed the fence and inched closer to the starving dog, speaking softly to it.

The dog growled but was too weak to pull against the chain to reach her. She eased closer, kneeled down, held her hand out for the dog to sniff it, and gave him a dog treat. He wagged his tail, and she moved closer and gave him another treat. She poured water in the palm of her hand, and the dog eagerly lapped it up. Darcy gently stroked his back and noticed that his collar was imbedded in the flesh around his neck. The poor dog would eventually choke to death if the collar wasn't removed. She wondered how anyone could be so cruel.

They probably chained him up when he was a puppy and threw some food out to him whenever they thought of it. By the looks of him, they didn't think about it often.

She softly said, "I promise I'll help you." She climbed over the locked gate, went around to the front door, and rang the bell.

Meanwhile, Officer Murphy sat at the monitoring system scanning the area in the mobile communication unit and was about to tell the sheriff all was clear for the SWAT team when he saw Darcy walk up to the target house. He shouted, "Chief, you need to see this."

Chief McKay leaned over Murphy's shoulder. "What's Darcy doing here? How did she get past the blockade?"

One of the ATFE agents stationed on a telephone pole spoke to Murphy via his radio microphone. "She was in the backyard with the dog before she came around to the front door. I saw her climb over the fence from the neighbor's yard behind the house."

Chief McKay pounded his fist into the palm of his hand. "Dammit! Get her out of there before she becomes a hostage or gets shot!"

"I'm on it." Scott had been standing next to him. He removed his police marked gear, shoved his Glock behind his back, and ran out of the mobile communications unit which was parked down the street. He briskly walked to the sidewalk in front of the gun dealer's house.

The door opened and revealed a large bearded man dressed in jeans and an undershirt with tattoos on his muscular arms. He scowled at Darcy as he shoved a bandana up higher on his forehead. "Whatever you're selling, I'm not buying. Get lost."

"I'm not selling anything. I'm with the Humane Society checking on an animal cruelty report pertaining to your dog."

Scott shouted, "Darcy, honey, please come here. I need to talk to you."

Darcy turned around and was surprised to see Scott. "Not until I finish talking with this man."

"Darcy, it's an emergency. I've been looking for you."

Her heart pounded as she ran to Scott, "Is my dad hurt?"

"No." Scott lowered his voice. "You're holding up a SWAT raid on this property. You have to come with me right now."

"No, the dog in the backyard might get shot. We have to save the dog."

Scott grabbed her arm. "We don't have time. We'll get him later."

"No!" She jerked her arm free. "I promised him." She was about to turn and walk back to the man standing at the door.

In one swift movement, Scott leaned down, scooped her off her feet, and slung her over his broad shoulder. As he strode away from the house, he said, "I don't have time to argue with you."

The man in the doorway yelled, "That's the way to handle women."

Darcy couldn't believe what was happening. "Put me down right now. Are you crazy?"

Scott ignored her pounding fists on his back and held her legs tight against his chest as he hurried down the sidewalk. Before he reached the Mobile Unit, he turned to see if the man at the house was still watching him. He wasn't. He had closed the door.

Scott set Darcy down inside the vehicle as she sputtered, "Let me go. I have to save that poor dog."

Chief McKay glared at his daughter and grabbed her hands. "Darcy, you stumbled into a SWAT raid on that house and everyone had to stand down until we got you out of there. Now be quiet while we get on with it."

"Dad, I'm sorry, but make sure they don't shoot the dog, *please*, Dad." Tears welled up in her eyes as she pleaded with him.

The chief spoke into a mike, "It's a go. And don't shoot the dog. I repeat, do not shoot the dog."

Darcy covered her face with her hands until she gained control of herself. She remained quiet and stood in a corner out of everyone's way.

The raid was successful. The ATFE agents confiscated all the guns without any bloodshed, handcuffed the gun dealers, and took them to jail.

"Please, Dad, can I get the dog now? I promised him I'd help him."

"All right, I'll tell them to let you through. Get your vehicle and drive it onto the driveway so you can load the dog into it. And be careful."

Darcy kissed his cheek and ran out to get her SUV.

Scott said, "She's going to need a bolt cutter to cut that dog's chain."

"We always carry one in this unit. It's in that cabinet behind you."

"I'll help her, Chief." Scott grabbed the tool.

The chief put his hand on Scott's shoulder. "Thanks … for everything."

Scott smiled. "Glad to help."

Scott was waiting for Darcy when she drove onto the driveway. "I'm here to help you with the dog. You keep him distracted while I cut his chain from the pole."

Embarrassed, Darcy blushed. "I'm sorry I yelled at you. Please accept my apology."

Scott put his arm around her shoulder. "Apology accepted. Let's get the dog."

She led the way. When the dog saw her, he wagged his tail, but then he noticed Scott behind her and growled.

"He doesn't trust men," she said. "Wait there and don't move until I get him turned around so he can't see you. When you cut the chain, leave enough attached to his collar so I can use it as a leash. I'll keep him busy eating so you can back out of the gate, okay?"

"Whatever you say."

"Thanks, Scott. I'll take him to Andy's Animal Hospital."

The dog was so hungry he didn't pay any attention to Scott when the chain was cut. Scott backed out and shut the gate. He listened to her sweet talk the dog as the dog wagged its tail and licked her face. Scott was impressed with her ability to gain its trust. He returned the bolt cutters to the cabinet in the mobile unit. The chief, Scott, and Murphy watched her load the dog in her SUV, wave at them, and drive away.

"At least we don't have to spend all day collecting evidence. The ATFE guys will handle that since this is a federal case." Chief McKay sighed. "We need to focus on catching Jennie's killer."

Murphy said, "I'll drive us back to the station."

THIRTY-ONE

That same morning Sandy Barker set about interviewing everyone who might help her write an accurate story about what had happened to Jennie Martin. Most of her freelance stories for the *Garnet Gazette* had been fluff pieces about things like beauty, pets, gardening, and the occasional charity benefit. This was her chance to do some serious journalism and maybe help catch Jennie's killer.

After interviewing Jennie's mother, the tow-truck driver, and the Uber driver, Sandy decided to drive out to Taylor Construction Company and interview Tom Taylor. He had been her boyfriend before Jennie had stolen him their senior year of high school, and Sandy remembered that he could be a jealous hothead. She decided to talk to him near employees, just in case he lost his temper.

Tom sauntered into the reception area. "Hello, Sandy, what brings you out here?"

"I'm working on a story for the *Gazette*, and I'd like to interview you." She gave him a big smile, hoping he'd cooperate. "I promise it won't take long."

He looked her up and down, pausing on her shapely figure. With a naughty glint in his eyes he said, "Anything for you, sweetheart." He glanced at the receptionist. "We'll be in the conference room. See that we're not disturbed."

"Oh, no, I wouldn't want to tie up your meeting room. Nobody's sitting out here." Sandy gestured toward a seating area in the reception lobby. "This'll only take a few minutes. Let's sit over there." She hurried to a chair facing a couch and sat down.

Tom followed her reluctantly and sat across from her. "What are you writing about?"

"Jennie's murder. As you probably heard, she was poisoned with cyanide before she was dumped into the lake. I'm interviewing everyone who saw her the day she disappeared, in case they remember something that might help solve the case."

"I was asleep in her bed when she sneaked out early that morning." Tom's eyes moistened. "She knew I didn't want her to go to that modeling interview in New York. If

I had taken her to the airport, she'd still be alive."

Sandy couldn't help noticing the bitterness in his voice and the genuine pain reflected in his eyes. "It wasn't your fault, Tom. If Jennie had survived that day, her killer would've found another way to get her. Any idea who might've done it? Did she have any enemies?"

He stiffened and looked into her eyes. "Only one enemy that I know of, and poison is commonly used by female killers. Where were *you* that morning?"

"Me? I'm not a murderer, and I have a verified alibi." She frowned. "How could you even think such a thing?"

"It's no secret you two have hated each other since high school, and I heard you were jealous Jennie got the modeling interview that you wanted." He sat back and crossed his arms, looking smug.

"That's not true. I enjoy my work at Dye to be Beautiful, and my freelance writing is very fulfilling. I thought I wanted to apply for a modeling interview, but then I changed my mind. I like living in Garnet." She stood. "Thank you for your time, Tom. Have a nice day." She turned and walked out the door before he could say anything else.

Sandy sat in her car and started the engine so the air-conditioning would run. She pulled out her cell phone and called the Calder residence.

Molly Calder answered. "Hello, Sandy. I saw your name on my caller ID. We're having another charity ball soon. Did you want to cover it? Is that why you're calling?"

"Actually, Miss Calder, I'm investigating Jennie Martin's murder for an article in the *Gazette*. I understand you found her body."

"Oh, it was dreadful seeing her floating face up beside my table at Betty's Bistro. I was lucky that handsome detective caught me when I fainted. Otherwise, I would've fallen into the lake right on top of poor Jennie."

"What a frightening thought." She paused. "Um, I'm following up on Jennie's modeling interview scheduled the day of the kidnapping. I think one of your neighbors owns Worldwide Modeling Agency in New York. Do you know him?" Sandy asked.

"Eric Stanton? Oh yes, sugar, he lives on the forty-acre lakefront property next door to ours at Two Lake Drive. He's a handsome bachelor in his mid-thirties and our only billionaire in Banyan Country Estates." She chuckled. "Eric's quite a catch. Would you like to meet him?"

"I'd love to. Do you think he'd see me if I drove out to his house right now?"

"I don't see why not. He enjoys meeting beautiful young women. I'll call him and tell him to expect you within the hour. And I'll notify the guard at our entrance gate."

"Thank you, Miss Calder. I really appreciate this." Sandy slipped her cell into her handbag and started driving to the Calder's exclusive lakefront community on the north side of Diamond Lake.

She stopped at the guard gate for Banyan Country Estates and showed her driver license and press pass. "Can you direct me to Two Lake Drive?"

The guard handed back her IDs. "Take the first left onto Lake Drive. The Stanton estate is the second home on the left side. The properties are large, so it's a few miles from here to his entrance gate. I'll let him know you're coming."

"Thank you." Sandy shoved her IDs into her bag and took in the view. Huge banyan trees, each looking like a small forest, lined the streets, providing welcome shade from the hot South Florida sun. A variety of flowering bushes and trees added lively colors to the manicured landscape.

Each home sat atop a man-made hill. The dirt came from digging deep canals to accommodate the residents who didn't have lakefront lots but wanted to keep their yachts docked at their homes. A network of canals connected each home to Diamond Lake, and the necessary bridges were high enough to allow passage of lake-going motor yachts but not sailboats. Watercraft with high masts used the nearby Garnet Marina.

Sandy admired the beautiful Arabian horses she spotted as she drove past the Calder estate. Another pasture on the opposite side of the street was home to a pair of palominos, their light-blond manes and tails blowing in the brisk wind.

Farther down the road, she pulled into the open entrance for Eric Stanton's property and checked her reflection in the pull-down mirror behind her sun visor. She pulled out lipstick and did a quick touchup. Then she ran a brush through her long blond hair. Satisfied, she parked under the porte cochère and exited her car.

A tall, fit man with black hair opened the front door. He wore tan riding breeches, black leather boots, and a white polo shirt. "Welcome to my home. I'm Eric Stanton. Molly said you're a reporter for the *Garnet Gazette*?"

"Yes, I'm Sandy Barker. Thanks for agreeing to see me on such short notice." She offered her hand, and he kissed it.

"Come in. I was just about to go riding, but I don't mind delaying it a little." He led her into a masculine living area furnished with comfortable chairs and sofas covered in soft brown leather. Large oil paintings depicted scenes from fox hunts and early America's Cup races. "Please, make yourself comfortable." He gestured to a mahogany coffee table with a crystal pitcher filled with brown liquid beside two tall glasses. "Sweet iced tea?"

"Thank you, I'd love some." She accepted a glass. "I know you're a busy man, so I'll get right to the point. I'm doing research for a story on Jennie Martin's murder."

Eric held up a hand. "Before I answer your questions, I'd like to know a little about my interviewer. Did you graduate college, Sandy?"

Surprised, she hesitated. "I, uh, I have an associate degree from Palm Beach State College and a beautician's license that I earned after graduating from Palm Beach Beauty Academy."

"And you're employed at the *Gazette*?"

"I work full-time at the Dye to be Beautiful salon in Garnet, and I write freelance articles for the local paper." Sandy took a sip of iced tea and tried not to look too long into Eric's penetrating blue eyes.

"Interesting. Did you attend Garnet High School?" he

asked, smiling.

"Yes, I earned straight A's all four years." She sneaked another peek at his handsome face and amazing deep-blue eyes.

"Did you have time for any extracurricular high school activities?"

"Four years on the cheerleading squad and in the chess club." She flushed. "I took second place in the state chess championship my senior year."

He sat back and studied her. "Beauty and brains, a rare combination. So, tell me, how can I help you?"

"Jennie said she had an interview with your modeling agency in New York. Did she schedule that through you?"

"I own many businesses in America and abroad, and I have people who handle the day-to-day running of each one. I just keep an eye on the bottom lines. Roger Sapphire is CEO of the Worldwide Modeling Agency. I'll give you his number so you can ask him who handles scheduling the model interviews." He glanced at his gold watch. "Will there be anything else?"

"Did you ever meet Jennie Martin? She worked at the Bodacious Buns Bakery."

"Can't say I've ever been in there—catchy name though." He stood. "Sorry I couldn't be more helpful, but I didn't know the murdered girl."

Sandy finished her iced tea and stood. "Thank you for seeing me, Mr. Stanton."

"Please, call me Eric. I hope you'll save me a dance at the Calder's next charity ball. I'll make sure they invite you."

"Thank you, I'd like that." She grinned like a silly school girl.

He kissed her hand once more and escorted her outside.

As she drove away, she spotted him in her rearview mirror as he mounted a black thoroughbred and cantered it into a grassy field.

Young, handsome, and rich—the trifecta of bachelorhood. If only—

THIRTY-TWO

Sandy drove home to her townhouse apartment in Garnet and sat in front of her laptop computer. Nothing clever came to mind since she hadn't learned anything new about the murder. Hardly the breakout article she'd hoped for. Too bad the article wasn't about the handsome bachelor she'd just met. She could happily write volumes about Eric Stanton's mesmerizing blue eyes, thick black hair, and hunky build.

Oh well, back to reality.

She sighed and called her friend, Detective Chuck Ryan.

"Hey, Sandy, what's up?" His voice sounded tired.

"I'm trying to write a story about Jennie's murder for

the local paper, but so far, I've got nothing to write that hasn't already been on TV. Any promising new leads?"

"Sorry, I've got nothing. We're assuming somebody from out of town just happened upon her—a crime of opportunity."

She straightened. "That can't be right. The chief told Darcy that Jennie hadn't been raped, and whoever kidnapped her left her purse and valuables behind for that construction worker to find. Hard to believe a stranger would drive around unfamiliar towns early in the morning, hoping to happen upon a victim."

"You're right. It doesn't fit," Chuck said. "The thing is, nobody local has a strong motive, and everyone local has an alibi. This is a tough one."

"Will you ask the guys working the murder with you if they'll cut me a break and give me first dibs on the story if there's a break in the case?" she asked. "Please?"

"Sure, but I wouldn't hold your breath. I gotta go, Sandy. Sorry I couldn't help you."

She glanced at her Timex watch. It was mid-afternoon.

My day off has been a total waste of time.

Her cell rang and snapped her out of her idle thoughts. The screen displayed Unknown Caller.

"Hello, this is Sandy Barker."

A deep voice that had obviously been altered by a speech device said, "Are you a newspaper reporter?"

"I write articles for the *Garnet Gazette*, why?"

"How'd you like a scoop on the Jennie Martin murder?"

"What do you know?" she asked, wary.

"I know who did it. I saw him take her," he said.

"Who was it?" she asked, pen poised.

"Not on the phone. Cell calls are too easy to intercept. I don't want to be his next victim."

"Meet me at Betty's Bistro," she said. "I'll get an outside table. There won't be a crowd this time of day."

"He's local. I don't want to risk him spotting me talking to a reporter. Meet me at the picnic tables in the wildlife refuge on the west side of the lake in thirty minutes, and no cops."

"Uh, I need more time," she said, stalling.

"Thirty minutes at the wildlife refuge or never. I'm already risking my life calling you."

"Why not tell the cops?"

"I'm a guy. If I tell them what I saw, they'll think I did it and arrest me. I want you to handle this. Thirty minutes." He hung up.

Sandy called Darcy. "You'll never guess what just

happened." She told her everything.

"You're not going, are you?" Darcy asked.

"I need this story." Sandy hesitated. "I was hoping you'd go with me."

"Let me think. We should go in separate cars so he doesn't get suspicious. I'll bring my dog posse with me, and we'll sneak up on him while he's talking to you. And I've got my Glock."

"Okay, but hurry. Now we only have twenty-five minutes to get to the picnic area up there."

"I'll call Dad on the way and tell him what we're doing," Darcy said. "It wouldn't hurt to have police backup coming if I have to do a citizen's arrest."

"Okay thanks, Darcy. See you soon."

Sandy grabbed her purse and keys and ran out the door.

She sped south and then west on Lakeshore Drive and entered the wildlife preserve through the south gate. No other vehicles were visible when she drove into the small paved lot for the picnic area. Were Darcy and the dogs hiding nearby, ready to pounce? She hoped so.

A fairly new white Ford F-150 pickup truck pulled into the lot next to her Toyota Corolla.

Her cell rang.

Unknown Caller.

She answered, "Hello?"

"I'm in the truck. Get in," he said.

"No, you get in my car. It's nice and cool," she said.

"Okay. Unlock your doors." An unattractive, stocky man in his mid-twenties with stringy hair and acne scars on his face jumped out of his truck and opened her car's door before she could change her mind. He slid into the front passenger's seat.

Sandy didn't recognize him, and his wild, ice-blue eyes scared her. She pulled out a note pad and pen. "Let's make this fast. What's your name, and who killed Jennie Martin?"

His right hand had been hidden by his side. He twisted around toward her and stabbed her thigh with a hypodermic needle. Before she could react, he pushed the plunger on the syringe and injected her with something.

In seconds, his face became blurry to her. Then total blackness set in.

* * *

Darcy was about six miles from the wildlife preserve when her left rear tire blew out. She pulled off the road and checked her watch. There was no way she could change the tire in less than fifteen minutes, which meant she'd be late coming to Sandy's aid. She tried calling Sandy's cell, but it went straight to voicemail.

Please, God, protect Sandy until I get there.

Darcy opened all the windows for her doggies and then rushed to change the flat tire. She was putting the jack back into the SUV when her dad pulled in behind her.

He joined her. "Flat tire?"

Darcy checked her watch. "Yeah, I just finished changing it, and now I'm fifteen minutes late meeting Sandy and her unknown source."

"Let's go. I'll follow you." Joe climbed into his police cruiser.

When she drove through the south gate, Darcy noticed the security camera for the entrance to the wildlife refuge had been smashed. She drove faster.

At first, relief flooded her when she spotted Sandy's white Toyota Corolla up ahead in the picnic area's parking lot. But she soon realized the car was empty, and no other vehicles were there.

She parked three spaces away to preserve the scene and rushed to the car, leaving her dogs in the SUV.

Joe was right behind her. "Don't touch anything." He

looked through the window. "It's empty, except for her handbag, and I don't see any blood. I'll pop the trunk."

He pulled on a glove, opened the driver's door, and hit the trunk release. "Nothing inside except a spare tire and a tool kit." He used his glove to open both front doors and turned to Darcy, who stood frozen in place, tears welling in her eyes. "Get the dogs. Tell two of them to follow the scent from the passenger's seat and the other two to follow the scent from where Sandy sat in the driver's seat."

Darcy sprang into action. She'd already tied the working bandanas on her dogs. She instructed Dobie and Tiny to take scent from the front passenger's side and follow it. Then she took Max and Laddie to the driver's side and told them to follow that scent.

In moments, all four dogs converged on the same area in the empty parking spot adjacent to Sandy's car. Dobie and Tiny sat where the driver would have entered his vehicle, and Max and Laddie sat six feet farther back on the same side.

Joe was already on his radio, calling in a forensic team and several police officers. He called the park ranger and learned the security cameras on the north and west entrances had also been smashed. The ranger said he didn't recall seeing anyone in the past hour, but he'd been busy mending a fence on the western border.

Darcy's dogs surrounded her as she sat on a nearby bench in the shade, softly sobbing. "She's dead, and it's my fault. If only I'd arrived on time."

Her dad gently squeezed her shoulder. "You don't know that to be true. She could still be alive, and if you'd been here, he might've taken you too."

"What am I going to tell her sister? Laura will never forgive me. And what about her parents?" Darcy moaned and covered her face with her hands.

Her dogs licked her and snuggled against her protectively.

Scott rushed up to her. "Don't worry, Darcy. We'll find Sandy. The entire force is looking for her. We found her cell phone in her purse, and we're checking with everyone she called today."

"What about the unknown caller? Can you trace his phone?" she asked.

Scott frowned. "We checked. It was a burner phone, and it's no longer functioning. He probably turned it off and threw it into the lake after he grabbed her."

Joe pulled her to her feet. "Honey, why don't you take the dogs home and feed them? There's nothing more you can do here. I'll call you if I learn anything new."

Darcy bit her lip. "Okay, Dad. I'm so sorry this happened."

"Again, not your fault. Go home and watch a movie with Sylvester."

She gathered her dogs and drove home as tears filled her eyes.

THIRTY-THREE

Two Weeks Later

Sandy Barker paced in a ten-foot-square room in what she assumed was a soundproof basement. Her little prison had an adjoining bathroom, no windows anywhere, and one metal door leading into a hallway. She held the heavy chain so it wouldn't drag on the concrete floor and cause the metal ankle cuff to dig into her skin as she walked. She glanced at her watch.

I'm not sure how long I was unconscious or how many days I've been here. Even though I've never seen my captor's face, I saw the guy who took me—probably his stooge. She paused. *What's he after? He hasn't raped or harmed me. We just play games every day. Chess usually, but sometimes backgammon, poker, or other card games. He always manages to win.*

The door lock rattled.

He's here.

She scurried backward into a corner as a tall man wearing a skeleton mask and a black silk suit entered carrying a white lace gown. Fit and toned, he moved like a cat.

He dropped the wedding dress on the bed. "Put this on." Tugging on crisp, white French cuffs, he adjusted his ruby cuff links.

Sandy stammered, "Are ... are we getting married?"

"No, dear, I collect bridal photos. You'll look lovely in this Vera Wang gown."

She sucked in her breath, edged forward, scooped up the gown, and shuffled into the adjoining bathroom, her chain chiming off the floor. She closed the door, but the chain held it open an inch.

He glanced at his gold Patek Philippe watch and selected "camera" on his cell.

A few minutes later, Sandy returned wearing the wedding gown.

"Good, now stand next to the painting on that wall and

smile." He held up a cellphone camera.

The smile she forced was more like a grimace. She trembled, terrified this would be her final act.

Her masked captor snapped a few pictures and checked them. "I'll be back later for our game." He left and locked the door behind him.

She glanced at her left ankle, sore from the metal cuff.

"Is this it? My last day alive? He imprisoned me for a few bridal photos?" she muttered to herself.

Once again, she surveyed her room. "What am I missing?" There seemed no way to escape. She closed her eyes. "God, please help me."

Can't quit. Think. All those thrillers I've read. The heroine always escapes. Must be something here that can help me.

She focused on a macabre painting by Salvador Dali. *The picture wire!*

She shuffled over to the painting and lifted it away from the wall. When she turned it around, she found a stout string stretched across the back.

"Darn!" She sucked in her breath and tried not to panic as she rehung the painting. *Maybe the bed springs.* She ripped open the box spring under the mattress and bent a small wire back and forth until it broke off. The wire punctured her finger, and blood dripped onto her expensive dress.

Using the short piece of wire as a makeshift lock pick, she struggled to move it just right in the ankle lock. *He could be back any minute. Must hurry!*

After fumbling with many failed attempts, she heard a crisp click, and her ankle cuff fell away.

She yanked the wire free and rushed to the metal door. Before she had a chance to try picking it, the lock clicked, and the door slammed into her, knocking her backward.

The man in the skeleton mask pushed her onto the bed. She kicked his muscular chest, hurting her bare feet. It had no effect on him. He snatched up the metal cuff and clamped it onto her left ankle.

"How dare you?" He grabbed the discarded wire and yelled, "Now you've made me angry."

Sandy scooted backward against the headboard, trembling as she looked into his murderous dark-blue eyes.

"This won't do." He pointed at her bloody dress and the blood spots on the sheets. "Shower off your blood. I'll arrange for band-aids, clean sheets, and a change of clothes." He grabbed her arm and yanked her from the bed. "Get in there, now!" He shoved her.

She reached for the shower control, her hand shaking, and selected a warm temperature. Stepping inside, she stood beneath the warm stream and let it soak her hair and dress. She moved slowly, letting the warm water help her recover.

It doesn't matter that I ruined the dress. He's going to kill me anyway.

When she finished stripping and washing, she wrapped a towel around herself and peeked into the bedroom. The bed looked lower.

Fresh sheets covered her mattress, and a clean Lilly Pulitzer dress and new underwear were draped across it. The box spring was missing.

Sandy eased into the room and glanced around. He wasn't there. Neither was the Dali painting.

She dressed quickly and hung the wet gown and towel in the bathroom after using the towel to dry off the chain. Tears ran down her cheeks as she sat on the edge of the low bed.

The door swung open, and her captor entered.

"Good, you're clean and dressed." He gestured to a chair. "Ready for a different game?"

He placed a checker board on the small table bordered

by two chairs. "You're an excellent chess player. Now let's see how you do at checkers."

She eased into the chair and touched the round game pieces with a shaky hand.

His dark eyes riveted on her, he pointed at the game pieces. "Red or black?"

"Black," she said in a weak voice.

"Good choice." He arranged the checkers on the board. "Remember, if you win, I'll free you, but if you lose, you're stuck here until you win a game." He waved at the black checkers, his ruby cuff links glinting in the light. "Your move."

"I'll do my best." Sandy tentatively moved a black piece forward.

As the game progressed, she managed to gain a slight lead.

He made his moves quickly, sometimes making errors that benefitted her.

Unnerved by his scary skeleton mask, she barely managed the courage to ask, "Will you really let me go if I win?" *Or will you kill me?* "I saw the kidnapper's face."

She took another red checker.

"My dear, I always keep my promises. Besides, the man who took you is long gone. He's not an issue." His next move took a black one of hers, leaving him behind by one. "Your move."

Sandy hesitated. *I should lose—allow time for his anger to cool. But what if he really will free me? I've never seen his face. He might let me go.*

Her final move lost the game, but just barely.

He kissed her hand. "Tough luck, my dear. Maybe next time." He glanced at his gold watch. "We won't share a delicious dinner, like we usually do after our games, because you must be punished for trying to escape." He stood. "If you want to go home, you'll have to win a game, fair and square. Think about that until our next match." He left and locked the door.

Home. I'd love to see my parents, and my sister Laura, and my best friend Darcy, and my other friends. I might've just missed my only chance.

She stared into the mirror as silent tears rolled down her cheeks.

That night and all the next day she went hungry. A bottle of water and a stale sandwich were delivered to her room for the evening meal.

He must still be angry, she thought as she ate the dry roast beef sandwich.

THIRTY-FOUR

The McKay Ranch

Darcy brushed Max's fur as she thought about Sandy and that it had been two weeks since she'd been kidnapped. Laura and her parents had been devastated, but they didn't blame Darcy, they blamed the kidnapper. Only Darcy blamed herself.

The Garnet Police had interviewed everyone Sandy had met with the day she was taken, but they didn't find anything that could lead them to her or her abductor. It was like she had vanished into thin air.

Darcy scratched Max's ears. "All done, big guy. You were last in line today." She kissed his nose. "Thanks for waiting your turn."

She gathered the grooming tools into their zippered bag and tossed the bag of shed hair into the garbage.

Her cellphone rang. It was her neighbor, Jane, who lived on the horse ranch next door.

"Darcy, I have a big jar of my homemade dill pickles for you. Our family is going on a picnic at the wildlife preserve, and I can drop it off on our way there. Will you be home?"

"Sure. You know how much I love your delicious pickles. When should I expect you?"

"In about twenty minutes."

"Okay. See you then."

They're going to the picnic grounds at the wildlife refuge—the last place where Sandy—don't think about it.

She swept the kitchen floor, killing time as she waited for Jane. A little later, she heard the doorbell.

"Hi, Darcy." Jane handed her a pickle jar decorated with a pink bow. "Thunderstorms are forecasted for later this afternoon so we want to hurry and enjoy our family picnic out at the lake. Seems like we hardly ever get a day off."

"Thanks a million, Jane, and have fun with Chris and the kids." Darcy hugged her and stood outside and waved as her neighbors drove away.

Jane and Chris work so hard taking care of their three children, ten horses, and managing the stables and trail rides. They deserve a break. I don't know how they do it all. Jimmy is eleven, Billy is nine, and little Marylou is only three.

Two hours later, Darcy received a frantic cellphone call from Jane. "Darcy, thank God I reached you. Marylou is lost in the forest! We've looked everywhere but can't find her. Can you please bring your dogs to search for her? A thunderstorm is closing in, and she'll be so frightened." Jane began to cry.

"I'll leave right now. Where are you?"

"We're in the picnic area at the wildlife preserve. Please hurry!"

Darcy put blue bandanas on Max, Laddie, Dobie, and Tiny. She kissed Daisy and said, "You stay here and keep Sylvester company. Your little legs are too short to be tramping through the forest."

Sylvester squawked, "I'll keep her entertained so she won't feel left out."

"Thanks, Sylvester."

"I'll expect a pile of my favorite crackers when you get back."

"Of course, you will." She sighed and loaded the eager

dogs into her SUV and raced to the wildlife refuge.

When she parked near the picnic tables, Jane and her family ran to her car. "Please find her before the storm hits."

"Do you have something with her scent on it?"

Jane handed her a small hat.

She held it in front of the eager dogs and said, "Take scent and find."

The dogs sniffed the hat and then sniffed the ground around them. They picked up her trail and ran into the forest, barking excitedly. Darcy and the family raced after them.

Darcy found a colorful pinwheel stuck in a bush where the dogs had stopped a short time later. "Is this Marylou's?"

"Yes," Jane said. "She was playing with it while I was preparing lunch."

"We have to find her before that rain storm moves in and washes away her scent trail." Darcy held the pinwheel in front of the dogs. "Search and find."

The dogs lifted their noses in the air and sniffed and then sniffed the ground. Thunder boomed in the distance as they raced deeper into the forest and began barking again.

Soon, they stopped barking and surrounded little Marylou as she lay sprawled on the ground crying. Laddie licked her face, and Max ran back to lead Darcy to the child while the other dogs guarded her.

Jane sobbed. "Why did they stop barking? Did they lose her scent?"

Darcy pointed at her German shepherd. "They found her. Look, Max came back to lead us." Darcy rushed after him.

The family ran behind her to where the dogs huddled around the child. Jane grabbed Marylou and hugged her tight. Lightning flashed as they all ran back to the parking lot with Marylou's daddy carrying her. She was crying and had scratches on her arms and legs, but other than that she was unharmed.

The family was relieved she'd been found so quickly. The parents hugged Darcy as they thanked her, and the boys petted and praised the dogs before the family got in their car and drove away.

Darcy petted her dogs. "Great Job! I'm so proud of you." She hugged them and gave them dog treats.

Before she drove home, she took a moment to say a prayer for her missing friend. "Please, God, help me find Sandy alive and safe."

THIRTY-FIVE

A Windowless Room

The man in the skeleton mask sat staring at the dead girl with the short blond hair seated in the chair across from him. *Number eighteen looks so peaceful now. I'll have Ray bury her.* He smiled. *My bridal gallery is almost complete. Once I deal with the other two girls, I'll have all twenty buried, well, except for the one Ray dumped in the lake. It's time to find a new hobby.*

He entered the adjacent room. "Hello, Tina, it's time for your bridal portrait." He handed her a white satin wedding gown trimmed with lace. "Put this on."

"Are we getting married?" she asked, her voice jittery.

"No, dear, I collect bridal pictures. After the photos have been taken, we'll play our usual chess game. Who knows? This could be your lucky day. Maybe you'll win and go home tonight."

Tina changed in the bathroom and emerged looking stunning in the beautiful gown. "This must've cost you a fortune. It's a Vera Wang."

"You're worth it, my dear." He pulled out his cellphone. "Stand over there beside the painting."

"You want this fabulous gown in the same photo with that horrid painting?" A look of revulsion clouded her face.

"I'm partial to it." He grinned and tapped his index finger against his cheek. "It goes well with my look, don't you think?"

"Why the mask?" She arched a brow. "Are you covering terrible scars, like the Phantom of the Opera?"

"I've worn this same mask down here for years, and you're the only one who's ever asked me about it." He paused, studying her. "Actually, I'm considered quite handsome, but if you saw my face, then I wouldn't be able to let you go, and you'd have no incentive to win the chess game."

"So ... if I win today, you'll let me go?" She studied his

dark blue eyes.

"Yes, my dear Tina. You should know after a month with me that I'm not a violent man, just lonely. Now, let's take that photo, shall we?" He waved toward the painting.

She stood with one hand caressing the skeleton face on the painting and smiled.

"Perfect!" He snapped several photos and then checked them. "I love the way you posed with the painting. It's the best photo in my collection." He grinned and slipped the phone into his pocket.

Before he could pull out her chair, she sat in front of the chess board and rotated it so that the black pieces were on her side. "You don't mind if we switch colors this time, do you?"

"Black might be your lucky color. Let's play. I'll even give you the first move."

She studied the board before she made her moves, while he seemed to move his pieces with reckless abandon.

Fifteen minutes later, she said, "Checkmate."

"Congratulations, Tina. I'll be back this evening with our dinner, and then I'll take you home." He grinned and left the room.

The door lock clicked into place.

THIRTY-SIX

Darcy delivered the missing poodle to its grateful owner and received a generous payment. She'd used Max, her German shepherd, to find the little dog who'd wandered away from home. The toy poodle's owner had been frantic with worry. Max sniffed one of the dog's toys and then tracked it a mile away where it was playing with another dog.

Thanks to that last-minute client, she earned enough money to pay the monthly installment on her bank loan. Andy's animal hospital was just down the street from the bank. After depositing the money, she decided to stop by the veterinary clinic and check on the pit bull she'd rescued.

Darcy was surprised to see Scott talking to Andy as she walked into the building.

"Your timing is perfect, Darcy," Andy said. "Scott's car broke down, and he needs a ride back to the station. I was going to take him, but I've been called out on a case."

"I'll give him a ride as long as he doesn't mind me making a stop first. I need to pick up a large donation for the Humane Society in Banyan Country Estates."

"I don't mind at all." Scott smiled. "I've heard a lot about that place and would enjoy seeing it."

"I know the sisters who built that exclusive community. They're charter members of the Humane Society. I want to tell them about the abused pit bull and ask if they want him."

"That's a good idea," Andy said. "I know they miss their old dog that died recently." He put his arm around Darcy's shoulder. "I'll call Mary and Molly and tell them you're on your way. The dog's neck will be healed soon. I know you'll want to bring him to them and explain his background. I hope they'll take him. He deserves a good, loving home after all he's been through."

As Darcy drove, Scott said, "Tell me more about the Calder sisters."

"They're twins from Texas. I think they're in their

sixties now. Their parents were ranchers, until oil was found on their property. They didn't need to raise cattle anymore to make a living, but they still raised horses. After their parents passed away, they inherited everything and married the Calder brothers who owned vast real estate holdings all over the United States."

Scott nodded. "When did they move to Florida?"

"A few years ago, after their husbands were killed when their private jet crashed into the mountains in North Carolina during a storm. The sisters were devastated and never remarried. They've taken over their husband's businesses and hired professionals to manage them. They built Banyan Country Estates here for people who want exclusive homes on several acres where they're allowed to have horses."

"It sounds like a great place."

"It has all the expensive amenities you'd find in a posh resort. There's a community center by Diamond Lake, boat channels to the lake, equestrian riding paths—you name it, they have it. They even have their own little town center with shops. The people who live there are wealthy down-to-earth people who don't put on airs. Not like some of the Palm Beach crowd. Mary and Molly are good friends of mine. Their only fault is they like to play matchmaker, especially for me."

"And have you met anyone you liked through them?"

"No, but they keep trying, and it's embarrassing."

THIRTY-SEVEN

Earl Stanton clipped some leaves off a special plant in his greenhouse. He was about to slip the leaves into a sandwich bag when a delivery truck pulled up with his exotic tree order.

He walked outside and said to the truckdriver, "The hole has already been prepared." He pointed. "Place it over there where my caretaker is waiting."

The driver nodded and pulled forward. Earl turned and walked back to his favorite poisonous plant. As he dropped the leaves into a plastic bag, he felt a breeze from the door opening behind him. He turned and faced a stranger.

"Hello, Stanton. It's taken me a long time to track you

down. For your sake, my daughter had better be alive."

Earl pulled out his cell. "I don't know who you are, but if you don't leave immediately, I'll call the police."

The man pulled back his suit jacket and pointed at a badge clipped to his belt. "I *am* the police, and you kidnapped my daughter. Where is she?"

Earl pocketed his phone. "I don't know what you're talking about."

"I think you do. That's why you didn't call the police. Now, where is she?"

"It might be helpful if you told me her name." Stanton smirked.

"Tina Trent, you know, the tall, willowy blonde you abducted from a modeling interview in your New York hotel suite a month ago." The cop drew his weapon. "That girl is my whole world since her mom died of cancer last year. I'll do whatever it takes to save her." He moved closer. "Tell me or I'll shoot you."

"*If* I have her, you'll never find her if you shoot me." Stanton grinned, enjoying the game as the delivery truck drove away.

"You misunderstood." He aimed at Stanton's right knee. "I'm not going to kill you—I'll just shoot you in painful, non-lethal places until you take me to my daughter. You have five seconds. One ... two—"

Stanton's cousin, Ray, crept behind the cop and hit his head with a shovel. The cop reflexively pulled the trigger an instant before he slumped forward unconscious. The bullet hit Stanton in the upper right side of his chest.

He staggered toward the door, trailing blood. "Ray, grab that tarp and wrap it around me so we don't leave a blood trail to the house. Take me up to the back terrace in the golf cart and carry me into my special room in the basement."

"Shouldn't I call an ambulance?" Ray asked, grabbing the tarp.

"No, I'll deal with the wound myself, and you'll come back here and bury the body in the hole where the new tree will be planted. I can call an ambulance later if the bleeding doesn't stop."

"Okay." He wrapped the tarp around Stanton and carried him to the cart.

THIRTY-EIGHT

Darcy showed her identification to the guard at the fancy entrance gate and drove in, enjoying the lush scenery and beautiful homes along the way to the Calder property. As Darcy drove up to the sprawling mansion, she saw Mary and Molly standing on the manicured lawn by the circular driveway, talking to a man. Molly smiled and waved as she pointed at the man with one finger and then at Darcy with her other finger, unobserved by her twin sister and the man.

Darcy heaved a big sigh. "She's letting me know they've found a man for me." I don't want to think about romance while my best friend's missing. "I'm calling in that favor you promised me. Consider us even if you pretend to be my boyfriend and let this poor guy off the hook."

Scott's blue eyes twinkled. "Never let it be said that Scott Logan refused to help a lady in distress. I'll do my best."

The Calder sisters seemed surprised to see Darcy with a man, a very handsome one. Then they recognized Scott from their encounter at Betty's Bistro the day they found Jennie in the lake.

Scott opened Darcy's door and put his arm around her shoulder as they walked toward the women with Max following them.

"Molly, Mary, I think you've already met my boyfriend, Detective Scott Logan, and you know my dog, Max. I see you have a visitor." She held her hand out to the stranger and introduced herself.

He shook her hand and then Scott's. "I'm Henry Osgood, and I'm glad to meet you." He adjusted his glasses and appeared ill at ease. "The twins invited me to Banyan Country Estates and wanted me to meet you, Darcy, seeing as how you're the president of the Humane Society."

Scott pulled Darcy close and kissed her cheek. "My little darling loves animals, and they love her." Scott gave

Darcy another kiss on her cheek and a hug. "Isn't that right, darling?"

Darcy forced a smile, nodded, and quickly turned away.

Scott halted her escape with a firm grip on her arm. He put his arm around her waist as they walked with the others to the house.

"Please stay for lunch. Our next-door neighbor, Earl Stanton, wants you to stop by his house afterward and pick up his donation for the Humane Society. Here's our check." Molly handed her the check as she smiled at Scott.

Mary put her hand on Scott's shoulder. "We're having barbecued ribs for lunch, Detective. I don't know any man who can resist that."

"My mouth's watering just thinking about it." He squeezed Darcy. "Please darling, let's stay for lunch and pick up that other donation on our way back to town."

Darcy agreed, and they all walked to an elaborate patio at the back of the mansion where the chef was busy brushing sauce on slabs of ribs. The aroma was enticing.

The conversation during lunch was pleasant and the food delicious. Darcy told them about her experience with the abused dog at the gun dealer's house, and the sisters agreed to take him as soon as his neck was healed.

Molly walked them to Darcy's SUV. "Earl Stanton lives about a half mile west on the next property on this side of the road. You can't miss it. His entrance gates will be open because he's expecting an exotic tree delivery. His house is built on a manmade hill like ours. His hill was made using the dirt from digging a deep pond for the horses on his forty acres."

Mary caught up with them and added, "Earl also has a large green house. One of his hobbies is collecting unusual plants and trees. He's handsome, single, and very wealthy. I'd guess he's about thirty-five. All the women are grateful he attends our balls."

Mary petted Max. "If you enjoy big band music, you should come to the next one as our guests. It'll be two weeks from today to raise money for the Garnet Library."

Darcy smiled mischievously. "Scott worked his way through college as a dance instructor and knows all the ballroom dances. I'm sure he'd enjoy teaching all the ladies."

Scott kissed her cheek and said, "Darling, you know I could never attend without you at my side." He glanced at the twins. "We'd love to come."

Darcy nodded. "Yes, thanks for the invitation. I'll make Scott wear a tux."

As they drove away, Darcy said, "Don't you think you went a little overboard with the boyfriend act, fawning all over me?"

"You wanted them to believe we're an item. That's what a boyfriend would do."

"That's a matter of opinion. Skip the boyfriend act around Mr. Stanton."

"You're the boss."

"I like the sound of that." Darcy drove through Eric Stanton's open gates toward the enormous mansion, even larger than the Calder estate. High atop a manmade hill, the house was set back from the long, curving driveway.

Darcy parked and glanced around. "Wow, I'm impressed! I wonder how many people he employs to take care of all this."

"He probably has quite a few with an estate this large." He opened the car door for her and bowed low with an elaborate flourish.

She laughed. "You're impossible."

After they let Max out, they walked to the front door. Scott pushed the ornate doorbell. They waited a few minutes, and he pushed the doorbell again. "That's odd. The twins said he was expecting us. I wonder why someone doesn't answer the door."

Max barked and ran along the front of the mansion. He rounded the corner to the back side of the home and continued barking.

Darcy and Scott caught up with her dog. He was sitting on the wide rear terrace near the lawn, staring at something on the tile.

"What did you find, Max?" Darcy asked. She looked at Scott. "Is that blood?"

"Looks like it, and it's fresh, but there's just a few drips. Maybe Stanton cut himself with a gardening tool." He opened the terrace door and listened. "I don't hear anyone, but it's a huge house." He yelled Stanton's name.

No one answered.

"Maybe Mr. Stanton went to the greenhouse to get a clipping from a medicinal plant. Let's go see," she said.

Max ran ahead and pawed at the main greenhouse door.

Darcy opened it, and Max ran into the large building filled with potted plants and trees. Long rows of narrow tables lined each side, with a wider table in the center.

The dog raced ahead, barking excitedly.

"Max found something he wants us to see," she shouted. His high-pitched barking told her it was urgent.

Scott pulled her behind him and drew his gun. "It

might be a wild animal or a poisonous snake. Stay behind me."

He walked slowly toward Max and spotted a trail of fresh blood leading to a side door. But the German shepherd was interested in something near the center aisle.

Max barked and sat. They found a man lying face-down behind some large sacks of potting soil. The back of his head bled from a wound and a bloody shovel rested on top of him.

Darcy kneeled down and pressed her finger against his neck. "There's a weak pulse. Better call an ambulance."

Scott called 9-1-1 and asked them to send an ambulance and the police. He looked at the unconscious man. "Darcy, have you ever met Earl Stanton?"

"No, but I doubt he'd wear slacks and a sport coat to work in a greenhouse." She reached under him and found a badge clipped to his belt. "He's a cop, and I think that's his Glock." She nodded at a pistol on the ground nearby.

"I'll check." He searched the man's pockets and found his wallet and official credentials revealing that he was David Trent, a NYPD detective.

Scott checked the weapon. "Recently fired. That explains the blood trail. Maybe he shot Stanton, but it looks like somebody hit him from behind with a shovel and knocked him out. Whoever hit him probably thought he was dead. Don't touch anything else. I'm calling in the crime-scene unit. They'll get fingerprints from the shovel and gun."

Darcy hugged Max, praising him. She took him outside and gave him dog treats from the plastic bag she always carried in her shoulder bag.

Scott shouted to Darcy, "I wonder how he got here. I didn't see a car parked on the driveway."

"I have a bad feeling about this." She pulled out her cellphone and called the Calder sisters. "Hi Mary, sorry to bother you, but do you know if Mr. Stanton lives alone?"

"His cousin, Ray, lives in the caretaker cottage, but he's not right in the head, you know what I mean?"

"Thanks, I'll explain later." She said through the greenhouse door, "Stanton has a cousin named Ray who lives on the property. Mary said he's mentally challenged."

"I'll request a search warrant, then I'll go look for Stanton and his relative."

"Do you want Max and me to help you find them?"

"No, one of them might be a killer. I'll wait for backup. In the meantime, I'll walk you back to your car so you and Max can go home."

An ambulance and several squad cars roared up the driveway, sirens wailing. Darcy and Scott rushed out and waved them toward the greenhouse.

Scott walked her and Max back to her SUV. "Can you and your furry friends come back tomorrow and help search the property if need be?"

"Search for what?"

"Don't know yet. I'll call you tonight."

THIRTY-NINE

When Darcy arrived home, Sylvester squawked, "It's about time you got here. We were worried about you. Tiny, Dobie, Laddie, and Daisy are upset because you left them home while Max was having all the fun."

"Where are they?"

"They're sulking under the dining room table."

Darcy walked over and kneeled next to them. "You might work tomorrow. Daisy will stay home and keep Sylvester company while we're gone. That is, if Scott calls and says he needs us." She hugged them.

They understood and showed her all was forgiven by licking her face and wagging their tails.

Sylvester ruffled his feathers. "Well, I'm glad you cleared that up. I need a snack ... please?"

"I think we all need a snack." Darcy handed Sylvester a cracker and gave the dogs milk bones. She drank a glass of milk, and ate three chocolate-chip cookies.

When her dad came home, he looked exhausted. She brought him a glass of milk and cookies. She gave him a hug and asked, "Did you find out anything about that unconscious NYPD detective?"

"I called his partner in New York. He said Dave was looking for his missing daughter, Tina, who was last seen going into a New York hotel suite for a modeling job interview."

"I wonder why he came to South Florida." She frowned. "Dad, do you know if the police need me and my dogs tomorrow?"

Her cell rang. "Hello? Hi, Scott, did you find Stanton and his cousin?"

His deep voice answered, "No, they seem to have vanished, but all their vehicles are on the property. Can you bring your dogs in the morning and help us search?"

"Sure, we'll need something from each man that has his scent. I'll see you in the morning."

The chief smiled. "Glad to see you're getting another job. You're well into your final month now. I hope it works out for you." He hugged her.

FORTY

Darcy drove her SUV with all her big dogs inside wearing their work bandanas to the Stanton estate. Officer Murphy met her on the driveway.

"I'm sure glad to see you," Murphy said. "We need all the help we can get." He directed her to the guest cottage where Scott had set up a temporary office.

Scott greeted her when she parked behind the mansion. "Glad you're here. We couldn't find anyone last night and thought maybe the cousin had gone somewhere overnight. I'm about to search the caretaker's quarters again for clues. Want to join me?"

"Sure, the dogs can get Ray's scent." Darcy and the dogs walked beside Scott down the back driveway toward the cottage, which was near a big maintenance garage at the bottom of the hill.

Darcy glanced at Scott. "Any news about the NYPD detective's condition?"

"The hospital told me he's still unconscious. I have Davis searching the contents of Stanton's office for anything he can find that might help us. The guy is a billionaire. He owns a well-known modeling agency in New York City, major companies in the US and in foreign countries, and loads of stocks and bonds."

Scott knocked on the cottage's front door. The house looked like a miniature version of the mansion. No one answered. "Obviously, we already searched every building last night, but Ray may have sneaked in later."

He opened the door, shouted, "Police," and then entered.

Darcy and the dogs followed. They searched the kitchen, three bedrooms and bathrooms, and a living room. The dogs took scents off dirty clothes in a bedroom hamper, just in case they caught his scent somewhere else.

"I'm surprised this cottage is so neat and clean," Darcy said. "You'd think he'd track in dirt from all the yard work he does."

"Well, there's nothing of interest here. Let's check out

the main garage next. It's attached to the east side of the mansion, and I'd like to see it again."

The garage wasn't locked. Scott reached for a light switch by the side of the door, and bright light filled the wide parking spaces.

He sucked in his breath. "Talk about a man with expensive toys." He ran his hand gently over the fender of a red Ferrari 488 GTB, smiling like a kid on Christmas morning, as he slowly walked down the line of fabulous cars and one of the most expensive SUVs ever made. He touched each one as he said its name reverently and took a photo with his cellphone. "This one's a Bentley Continental GTC, and that one's an Aston Martin Virage, and here we have a Rolls Royce Ghost, and my favorite, this black McLaren 720S Spider, and then a Lamborghini Aventador, and finally a Range Rover Autobiography." He heaved a big sigh as he put his hand on his chest, "Be still my heart."

Darcy shook her head. "Men and their toys." She nudged him. "You must be a huge fan of high-end cars to know the names of each one."

Scott smiled and waved at the vehicles. "These aren't just cars, they're works of art. My team will go wild when they see them. I might have to post a guard here."

Next, they walked back down the hill and entered a huge maintenance garage and workshop. It housed all the heavy vehicles and machines that kept the vast estate in tip-top shape.

Scott was filled with admiration as he glanced around. "This is every man's dream. Look at all the machinery and top-of-the-line tools."

All the heavy equipment, including a big tractor and a backhoe, were parked in neat rows on the concrete floor. A long workbench ran along one wall with numerous tools neatly hung above it.

Scott was inspecting the workbench and the tools when Darcy noticed a white Ford F-150 pickup truck parked near the tractor.

She opened the passenger side of the truck and looked inside the glove compartment. A leather folder held the vehicle registration and a paper copy of a driver license with a photo of the driver. "Hey, look at this." She handed it to Scott.

He examined the information. "This is Ray's truck. According to the driver license, Ray Stanton is twenty-six."

Scott glanced around. "Where *is* he? Yesterday, he wasn't in his cottage or the mansion, and it looks like all the vehicles are here. This case is frustrating. We've got that unconscious detective in the hospital, Stanton's missing, and so is his cousin."

She took his arm. "We need some fresh air, and so do the dogs."

The dogs were happy to be outside and ran circles around them. Darcy noticed that Laddie began sniffing the ground. He flattened his ears, put his tail down between his back legs and crawled on his belly under a large bush. He backed out, scratched at the ground, looked back at her, and sat down.

Dobie, Tiny, and Max trotted over to Laddie. They sniffed the ground and sat beside him.

As he watched the dogs, Scott frowned. "I don't think this case can get any worse."

Darcy sighed, put her hand on his broad shoulder, and softly said, "I'm sorry, but it just did."

He glanced at her. "What do you mean?"

"Laddie found a buried body."

He shook his head. "Awwww, no. Are you sure?"

She nodded. "That's what they do to alert me when they find a body. The nose always knows."

FORTY-ONE

Scott ran his hand down his face. "Okay, I'll go inside and tell two of my men to get shovels from the greenhouse and start digging. And I'll get the ME back out here."

Darcy praised the dogs and gave them treats. Then she sat on the grass near them to wait for the police to take over.

Two unhappy officers arrived carrying shovels. One of the men said, "I'm Officer Jim Cassidy." He pointed at his partner. "That's Officer Ken Davis. Detective Logan ordered us to dig for a body your dogs discovered."

"Yes, it's right there." She pointed to where the dogs waited. "Laddie, Dobie, Tiny, and Max, come here." The dogs trotted to her and watched the men as they dug.

After they had dug an area the size of a grave and about twenty inches deep, Jim frowned, wiped his brow, and leaned on his shovel. "Are you *sure* there's a body here?"

She nodded. "I'm sure. Keep digging."

The men grunted and continued. When they had dug deeper, a shovel blade clanged against something hard.

The dogs gave a sharp bark.

Darcy said, "Better use your gloves to move the rest of the dirt. I think you've hit a bone."

Both men got down on their knees and pushed the dirt aside, revealing a skeleton.

"I'll never doubt the dogs again," Jim said as he stood and brushed the dirt off his pants.

Don Jackson, the robust, gray-haired medical examiner arrived. He was in a good mood, despite the circumstances. "Darcy, we have to stop meeting like this. People are beginning to talk."

She smiled and gave him a hug. "I bet you tell that to all your girlfriends."

He grinned. "No, only you, because you keep me busy." He checked the skeleton. "I think it's a young adult female, but I'll know more when I examine the bones in my lab."

"It's not Sandy, is it?" she asked, afraid of what he

might say.

"Not possible. This one has been here at least a few years—nothing but bare bones."

"Good. Well, don't work too hard." She waved and headed back to the cottage. When she noticed her dogs weren't with her, she stopped.

Glancing around, she gasped when she spotted them. All four dogs were sitting in separate areas, alerting her they'd found more bodies. She walked to each one, praised him, ordered him to stay, and gave him a treat. Then she went back to inform the men.

Ken and Jim leaned on their shovels while talking to Don.

"Well, I'm glad were done with the digging," Jim said.

"Yeah," Ken said. "It's too hot. Let's get a cool drink."

Darcy overheard them. "Guy's, I'm really sorry, but my dogs found four more bodies. After we mark the spots and get cold drinks, you might want to get help digging them up. And there could be more out there. I'd better have the dogs search the whole area."

Disheartened, Jim and Ken hung their heads and picked up their shovels. Jim walked over to Laddie and stuck his shovel in the ground next to him to mark the grave site. Ken did the same for Dobie's find, Don marked

Tiny's spot with a latex glove stuck partly into the ground, and Darcy took care of Max's find by jamming a stick into the grass.

She walked to the caretaker's cottage with the men and her dogs.

Inside the kitchen, she put bowls of water on the floor for the dogs and then enjoyed ice water with the men as they sat at the kitchen table, resting.

Scott walked into the kitchen with a puzzled expression. "Are you finished digging up the body?"

Jim stood. "Yes, Detective, but we needed some cold water before we start digging up all the other ones."

He frowned. "What other ones?"

Ken stood next to Jim and said, "Her dogs found four more bodies."

"Actually, they're probably skeletons, like the first one they dug up," Don said.

Scott closed his eyes, and slowly shook his head.

Darcy put a hand on his shoulder. "I'm sorry, but there could be more graves out there. I'll stay and have the dogs keep searching."

Don leaned against the kitchen counter. "Looks like I'll be here for a while, Scott. This property could be a burial site for a serial killer. First, let's take a lunch break.

I'm hungry, and I'm sure your team is too. I'll order pizzas and cold drinks."

The men working in the other room heard Ben mention pizza and walked into the kitchen. "Count us in."

All the guys nodded in agreement.

After everyone had lunch, Darcy had the dogs resume the search. The hot afternoon sun beat down on them as they slowly discovered two more burial sites. She returned to the cottage's kitchen to get cold water for the dogs.

Scott greeted her. "How's it going out there?"

"I need something to mark the graves." She dropped into a chair and drank a cold glass of water.

His jaw dropped. "How many?"

"Well, we're not finished, but we just found two more burial sites. I need to take cold water to my dogs. They're waiting at their finds."

An officer seated nearby said, "I found several cans of white spray paint in the maintenance garage. Can you use them to mark the grave sites?"

"Spray paint is perfect—easy to use and durable. Thanks!" Darcy grabbed a gallon jug of cold water and her dog's bowls. "Scott, can someone bring the paint to me? I need to water the dogs."

"Sure, I'll get one and take it to you."

FORTY-TWO

It took almost three hours for Darcy's dogs to find two more graves. She and her furry helpers were overheated and exhausted.

Scott found her spraying an X on the second site. "That's enough searching today. You and the dogs look like you're about to collapse. You've been out in the hot sun too long and might get heat stroke. Go home and rest. The graves will still be here whenever you feel up to continuing the search. But come in first and drink some cold water."

"Okay." She stumbled and would've fallen, but Scott caught her. The dogs followed as he carried her inside and set her in a chair. He handed her a tall glass of cold water and poured cold water into the dogs' dishes.

Her hands shook when she gulped down the cold drink.

He sat beside her. "Rest until you feel strong enough to walk to your SUV."

Scott called to Officer Murphy, who was working on a computer in the living room.

Murphy walked in. "What do you need?"

"Drive Darcy and her dog's home in her vehicle and have Jones follow you to bring you back here. She'll be ready to go in a few minutes."

Darcy was too tired to object. Scott handed her a cold wet cloth to put on her neck while she rested and cooled down.

* * *

The next day, Darcy's Sniffers Agency was back on the job. The dogs found eight more graves for a total of seventeen burial sites on the property. She used the spray paint to mark the graves.

"We have a serial killer at work here. Is it Eric Stanton or his cousin?" Don asked Scott.

Scott shrugged. "I don't know, but that's what I'm

determined to find out." He had to call for reinforcements to carefully handle and load the skeletons and cadavers under Don's directions into numerous vehicles to take to his laboratory so he could thoroughly examine them. Don was determined to find out who they were and how they died. Everyone involved with the case felt depressed about finding so many graves and were anxious to hear the results.

Chief McKay called in the FBI to help identify the bodies and catch the killer.

"We need to find Eric and Ray Stanton. I think Ray knows about the graves since he's the caretaker here," Scott said.

Darcy frowned. "Do you think he's hiding somewhere on the estate?"

Scott nodded. "He must know this property inside and out like his wealthy cousin."

Darcy smiled. "I have an idea."

"Tell me about it. I need all the help I can get."

"I'll use Max and Dobie. The other dogs can rest. I need something Eric Stanton has worn, preferably from his clothes hamper. The same for Ray. My dogs will be able to track their scents. We'll do a search and find drill and search the whole mansion and grounds if necessary.

If they're still here, we'll find them."

Scott said, "Thanks. You just brightened my day."

She smiled, "I'm happy to help."

"I'm posting guards inside and out until you get back."

Darcy gave him a salute. "Expect us in an hour." She grinned as she left.

FORTY-THREE

An hour later, the officers on guard duty welcomed Darcy, her German shepherd Max, and Dobie, her Doberman. They were led into the opulent mansion.

Scott glanced at his watch. "That was fast. Are you ready to search?"

The dogs barked and she nodded. "Where do you want to start?"

Scott handed her a soiled work-shirt he'd found in Ray's hamper and a dress shirt with smelly armpits from Eric's hamper. "These should have good scents on them. Want to start on the second floor and work your way down, or do you have another way you think would work better?"

"We'll start at the top and work our way downstairs. These shirts are perfect for tracking them. Thank you."

"I'll accompany you in case you find them," he said.

Scott, Darcy, and her dogs climbed the tall, ornate staircase to the mansion's second floor instead of taking the small elevator. Darcy held the shirts under the dogs' noses and gave the command, "Take scent, find, and hold."

They sniffed the shirts and then sniffed outside the first bedroom in the long, carpeted hallway. Scott looked through the open door. The dogs sniffed the floor but didn't find a scent so they turned back into the hallway.

"How many bedrooms are up here?" Darcy asked.

"There's six guestrooms plus the master suite," Scott replied.

Moving quickly with their noses to the floor, the dogs checked each open bedroom door and moved on down the hallway.

Scott stepped in and looked around one of the lavishly furnished rooms. "Are you sure the dogs are doing a thorough job? Shouldn't they search inside every room?"

Darcy sighed. "Their noses know. I trust them."

Scott shrugged. "You're the boss."

The dogs bypassed all the guestrooms and continued

to the master bedroom at the end of the long hallway. It was much larger than the other rooms, covering both sides of the house.

Max perked up a little, sniffing around the massive antique four-poster bed. He followed a scent to the huge walk-in closet and then sniffed around inside the master bath.

"Look at all the hand-carved work in this furniture," Scott said.

Darcy nodded. "Do you think it came from a royal family?" Filled with awe, she glanced around. "I've never seen a bedroom suite this elaborate."

Max and Dobie were anxious to get back to work. They put their right front paws on her leg.

"Okay, we'll get going." She petted them and turned back to the hallway.

"Wait," Scott said. "I thought Max picked up Eric's trail."

"This is Eric's bedroom. Max caught a light residual scent from a while ago. Nobody is on the second floor today except us."

The dogs trotted down the steps to the main floor with Darcy and Scott close behind them.

"Well, let's hope they're somewhere down here in a

secret room," Scott said. "Do you mind if we check the basement before we search the huge main floor?"

"No problem. Where is it?" she asked.

"This way." He led her and the dogs to the basement steps.

The basement was an elaborate wine cellar that held at least a thousand bottles of various vintages and varieties.

Darcy had the dogs check for a secret room. The walls were solid concrete covered with stone bricks. "Nothing here," she said. "Let's search the main floor."

They entered the large living room and admired the soaring twenty-foot coffered ceiling, crystal chandeliers, huge fireplace, and expensive antique furniture.

"This mansion must have cost a fortune to build with all the marble and hardwood floors and the hand-carved wainscoting and arched window frames," Darcy said.

Max and Dobie led them to the dining room. While they gazed at the expensive paintings, the dogs sniffed the floor around the chairs at the massive mahogany table.

The dogs lost interest and moved on to the kitchen with its custom wood cabinetry. It had granite counter tops, stainless-steel appliances, a large breakfast nook, and a butler's pantry.

Darcy said, "I'd enjoy cooking in here."

The next room was a large home theatre.

"This would be heaven for watching football games," Scott said.

The dogs quickly checked all the reclining seats and then continued on to a large gym filled with expensive exercise equipment.

"This guy thought of everything. He bought the whole candy store," Scott said.

Max and Dobie weren't impressed and continued to the library. They sniffed the floor along the huge built-in bookcases and ignored the comfortable furniture arranged in front of a huge fireplace. Not finding either man's scent, the dogs sniffed the air and raced into Stanton's office. Both dogs barked and lunged at a floor-to-ceiling bookcase along one office wall. They sat on the floor and stuck their noses against a book near the end of the third shelf from the bottom. They whined, looked at Darcy, and pressed their noses on the book again.

She read the book's spine, "Huh, it's *The Complete Tales and Poems of Edgar Allan Poe*. And there's blood on it. Creepy." She pulled out the black leather-bound book and found a hidden handle recessed into the wood.

Scott's jaw dropped when she pulled the handle, and

the entire bookshelf swung open and revealed a stairway leading downward. She handed him the book.

Scott said, "The dogs found the secret room. Wait while I call my team for backup." He stepped back to make a cell call, and the dogs rushed down the stairs.

Darcy yelled, "No!" and rushed after her beloved dogs, worried the killer might hurt them.

A loud thud sounded behind her.

FORTY-FOUR

She used the flashlight in her cellphone to light her way. The stairway emptied into a dark hallway with three bolted doors along one side and another door at the end. The dogs eagerly sniffed at all the doors.

Darcy unbolted the first door, exclaimed, "Oh, my God!" and put her hand over her mouth. In the darkness, she could barely see a young woman lying on a bed with her ankle chained to the frame.

"Max, Dobie, heel!" Her dogs instantly appeared at her sides and entered the room with her. They sniffed the woman who hadn't moved or made a sound.

Darcy eased closer with her cell light and recognized the face. "Sandy!" She checked for a pulse and barely detected one. "Scott, get in here!"

What's taking him so long?

Sandy was alive, but unconscious. The chain connected to her ankle was long enough to reach a small bathroom near the bed. Darcy bent over the ankle clasp and tried the many keys on her keychain, hoping one would trip the lock. She was so focused on the ankle lock she didn't notice that her dogs had moved away from her.

She sensed someone behind her and assumed it was Scott. She turned and looked up.

A stocky man loomed over her holding an eight-inch hunting knife. His face matched the driver license she'd found in the pickup truck. Ray Stanton. He raised the knife and said, "One more for Eric's collection!"

Trapped against the bedframe, Darcy had nowhere to escape as the knife arced down toward her.

Glowing eyes appeared on either side of her attacker. Max's powerful jaws closed around the wrist wielding the knife, his canine teeth sinking deep into the flesh. Equally powerful jaws clamped down on Ray's other wrist as the fierce dogs pulled him to the floor.

Ray's feral screams echoed into the hall as the dogs' jaws held him in vise-like grips, blood from his severed arteries pooling under him.

Scott burst into the room with several men behind him. His flashlight played across the scene. Darcy's face and chest were splattered with blood. "Oh no, Darcy, are you hurt?"

"I'm fine, but Sandy is barely hanging on to life. What took you so long?"

"The door shut the instant you ran down the steps, and I couldn't get it to open again. I finally figured out that the book had to be put back to reset the lever, something that I guess they usually did before they went down the stairs."

She glared at Ray and asked Scott, "Should I call off my dogs or let this monster bleed out?"

"Call off the dogs. We might need him alive." He tore strips from his shirt to tie off the blood loss, and someone on his team called for paramedics.

They checked the other two rooms and found another young woman in the same condition as Sandy, and an empty third room.

Dobie stayed to protect Darcy while Max's growling drew their attention to a closed door at the end of the hallway. He scratched at it and barked.

The men drew their weapons.

Scott shouted, "Eric Stanton, come out with your

hands above your head."

Darcy said, "Max, stand down." He immediately came to her side.

There was no answer.

Scott shouted, "If you don't come out right now, we'll break the door down." Scott grabbed the door handle and the door swung open. A dim ceiling light revealed Eric Stanton's dead body stretched out on a hospital bed. Blood-soaked bandages covered a gunshot wound in his chest. The odor indicated he'd been dead a while, probably since the day Detective Trent from New York had shot him.

Darcy put her hand over her nose and turned away.

The men shook their heads and holstered their weapons.

Scott said, "I wonder who the hangman's noose was for?" He pointed at a noose tied to a ceiling beam. A chair was positioned beneath it.

He called the crime scene unit and the medical examiner. Then he told the officers with him, "Look around the room and see if one of them left a note."

Darcy walked over to a desk and found a letter addressed to the police. She handed it to Scott. It read: *My name is Ray Stanton. My cousin was my guardian.*

He gave me a nice place to live, and I got to drive all his vehicles. I helped him hide his crimes and buried the women he killed, except for the one I tossed in the lake. I'm not sorry I helped him, but he's dead now, and I don't want to go to jail. I'd rather die. You'll find evidence of his greatest work in his office safe. When you cut me down, bury me beside my cousin.

Scott took pictures of the two girls before they were carried out by the paramedics—more evidence against Ray and Eric.

Darcy hugged her dogs and led them upstairs. "Good dogs. You saved my life." She fed them treats and petted them.

When the paramedics rushed by her carrying Sandy, Darcy prayed her friend would survive.

The medical examiner patted Scott on the back. "The chief is lucky to have a daughter like Darcy, and her dogs are awesome. You should take her to dinner."

Scott nodded. "She's one of a kind all right."

A locksmith arrived and opened the office safe. It was filled with completed modeling applications and all the bridal photos that helped identify the missing girls.

"Hey," Scott said. "One of the girls Eric took was Tina Trent. The man in the hospital is Detective David Trent who was looking for his daughter, Tina."

"Is Sandy in one of the bridal pictures?" Darcy asked.

Scott checked the bridal photos. "Yep, good thing you found her in time." He smiled at Darcy and gave her a thumbs-up sign.

"I'm glad the detective's daughter is alive too. Maybe they can be in the same hospital room. Have you heard how Detective Trent is doing?"

"He has a concussion, but he's awake now. I can't wait to tell him the good news." Scott pulled out his cell and called the hospital.

Everyone was in a better mood after finding two girls alive.

Darcy gave her dogs more pats on their heads. "You did very good jobs. I'm so proud of you."

They licked her cheeks, and she drove them home where she fed them delicious dinners.

FORTY-FIVE

The next morning her cellphone rang early. "Hello."

"Darcy, this is Chuck. I need you and one of your furry friends to help me find a missing fisherman on Diamond Lake. Can you meet me at the marina?"

"I'll meet you at the boat docks. I just got up. Give me an hour to take care of my dogs, and I'll bring my Labrador to do the search."

When Darcy met Chuck, he said, "The family told me the missing man is in his seventies and has a heart condition. They think he might have had a heart attack and fell out of his boat and drowned. The boat with his fishing gear was found partly grounded on shore."

"Is that the man's family sitting at the picnic table?"

Chuck nodded.

Darcy and Laddie went to the family. "I'm so sorry about your missing family member."

Six people were seated at the picnic table, and four of them were talking on their cellphones.

A woman stood up. "Thanks for coming to help us find him. My dad loved fishing. It's the only sport he was able to do because of his heart condition. He's been missing for almost two days." The woman choked back a sob, and covered her face with her hands.

Darcy laid her hand on the women's shoulder. "We'll do our best to find him."

She walked to the missing man's rowboat and let Laddie sniff a few of the items in the boat to get the man's scent. "Take scent and find."

Laddie gave Darcy a soft woof to let her know he was ready to work.

Confident they'd find the man's body, Chuck watched Darcy and Laddie work.

Laddie sniffed the ground along the shoreline north of the boat. He walked about a hundred yards and sat with his nose in the air. He turned and stared across the lake.

"Chuck, we need to get in a boat and head out to where Laddie is looking."

He used his cellphone to contact the officer and scuba diver that had been searching for the drowning victim. When they docked, Chuck, Darcy, and Laddie got into the low boat with them.

She pointed southwest. "Head out there."

The diver grumbled, "We've already searched that area and didn't find him. Are you sure your dog knows what we want him to do?"

Darcy nodded. "His nose knows. I trust him."

No one spoke as they stared ahead. They were out in the middle of the lake when Laddie lowered his head over the side, sniffed the water, and then scratched at the bottom of the boat.

"Stop here and drop anchor," Darcy said.

The diver rolled his eyes and frowned. "You want me to search here *again*?"

She gave him a nod. "Don't worry, this time you'll find him."

"I doubt it, but you're the expert." He adjusted his gear, leaned backward, and rolled into the lake.

In a short time, he surfaced and pulled out his mouthpiece. "I don't believe it. He's down there. The current must've carried him here after we searched this area. His clothing is caught on a sunken tree branch. Get the body bag ready. It'll take me a few minutes to cut him free." He put his regulator back in his mouth and dived under the boat.

Chuck smiled and said to the other officer, "I told you they'd find the body."

The diver surfaced with the cadaver, and Chuck and the other officer helped lift it into the boat.

Darcy hugged Laddie and praised him. Then she gave him some treats she always carried with her.

Chuck phoned the M.E. to meet their boat when they arrived back at the pier.

When they docked, the dead man's nephew identified him. His family thanked Darcy and petted Laddie, saying, "Good dog."

Laddie wagged his tail and then went for an exuberant swim in the lake before Darcy could stop him.

"Oh well, Labradors love to swim, and he earned it." She pulled a big towel out of her SUV and dried him off after he had a good shake.

Chuck smiled. "I knew you and your furry friend would find the victim when all else failed." He put his arm around her shoulder. "Well done, my friend."

FORTY-SIX

When Darcy arrived home, Silvester reported, "Everything has been quiet on the home front.

"Good. I've had enough excitement in the past few days to last me a long time." She pulled out the treat bins. "Anybody want a biscuit or a cracker?"

The dogs barked, and Sylvester said, "I always want a cracker. You know that."

She handed him a cracker and then passed out biscuits to all the dogs.

Sylvester squawked. "The chief is home."

Darcy glanced out the kitchen window and spotted her dad walking to the door.

She hugged him. "Hi, Dad, how was your day?"

"A lot better than the days before you solved the Stanton case. And I heard you and Laddie found a DB in

Diamond Lake for Detective Ryan. Well done."

"Thanks, Dad. Too bad our police station doesn't have the budget to pay me more for my work. My dogs found seventeen bodies, plus two live girls, one unconscious detective, one live perp, and one dead one on Stanton's estate. But I only earned a hundred dollars per person found. That was about twenty-six hours of work over three days with all four big dogs and only $2,200 for my trouble. Hardly seems fair. I'll get another hundred for today. Big whoop."

"You're right, it isn't fair, but that's all the department can afford. Add to that all the pro bono cases you accept, and it's no wonder you never make a profit. Face it, honey, this isn't working out financially, and I don't make enough money to keep funding your Sniffers Agency. I'm sorry, but your time's up. Time to close your business."

"But look at all the good my agency does. Your detectives would have had a really tough time solving that Stanton case without me and my dogs."

He sighed. "That's true, but eventually they would've solved it."

"Maybe, but not soon enough to save Sandy or Tina."

"I agree, but there's nothing more I can do." He hugged her. "Sorry, honey."

FORTY-SEVEN

That night, Scott took Darcy to an Italian restaurant after they stopped at the hospital to visit Sandy, who was recovering steadily. At the restaurant, Darcy put on a brave face, and they made small talk for the first thirty minutes, discussing their day.

She looked into his brilliant blue eyes and smiled. *He's so handsome. I wouldn't mind seeing him at the police station every day if I got a job there.*

Scott looked into her moist green eyes. "You look sad. Is there something you're not telling me?"

She looked down at her plate. "Dad and I had a chat about my business. He reminded me I'm pretty much out of time. The deadline is tomorrow."

"My offer is still good. Let me get a loan and help you

keep your company."

"No, thank you, but it means the world to me that you offered."

"I understand." He took her hand and kissed it. "I love spending time with you, Darcy. We have so much in common."

"I admit I had my doubts." She hesitated. "I had my heart broken by a guy in college who was handsome like you."

"Not all good-looking men are heart breakers." He gazed into her emerald-green eyes. "Honestly, I'm not a player. I just want one good woman—you."

She reached out and squeezed his hand. "I've been thinking about you, and I've decided we should give it a try—that is, dating exclusively—if you want to."

He grinned and kissed her hand. "Count me in, girlfriend. Let's go for a walk in the moonlight."

They strolled hand-in-hand on a paved path along the lakefront.

Scott stopped under the shadow of a banyan tree and drew her to him. He lifted her chin and kissed her deeply.

Wow, he makes my heart race. It's been a long time since I've been this excited about a man. I wonder if he's the one.

FORTY-EIGHT

The next day, Darcy paced as she waited for her father to get home from work. He pulled into the driveway at 4:30 p.m.—not a good sign.

"The chief's home early," Sylvester announced.

"I hope it isn't because something bad happened or he's already got a buyer for some of my agency's equipment." She opened the kitchen door, and the dogs rushed out to greet him.

She pulled a cold beer out of the refrigerator and handed it to him when he walked through the door.

He hugged her. "Looks like I'm getting the royal treatment."

"You're home early. Is everything okay, Dad?"

"Got any cookies?"

"I made a big batch of chocolate chip cookies this afternoon. They're in the cookie jar. Why? Is something wrong?"

"Sit down." He grabbed the cookie jar, two glasses, and a quart of milk.

"Dad, you're scaring me. What happened?"

He poured the milk, put it back in the refrigerator, and grabbed two plates. "Don't worry, it's nothing major. Relax and have some cookies." He dipped one in his glass of milk.

Darcy inhaled two cookies. "Okay, now tell me." She drank some milk.

"Garnet P.D. won't have any openings for a year or two—budget cuts. But they have openings over in West Palm Beach. You can get a position there after you graduate from the police academy."

"I told myself losing my Sniffers Agency wouldn't be so bad because I'd get to see Scott at work every day. Now that won't happen either." She frowned and ate two more cookies.

"Unknown vehicle pulling into the driveway," Sylvester announced as the dogs rushed to the door.

McKay looked out the kitchen window as a man exited a white Mercedes sedan. "I recognize him. That's Matt

Sorensen. He's a lawyer with the biggest law firm in Palm Beach. You've probably seen their commercials on TV."

"Yes, but what's he doing here? I hope I'm not getting sued."

McKay turned to the dogs. "Stand down." He glanced at the parrot. "Zip it until we find out why he's here."

"Whatever you say, Chief."

He opened the door. "Hello, Matt, what brings you out to the boonies?"

"I have business with your daughter." Matt glanced at her. "Are you Darcy McKay?"

"That depends. Am I in trouble?"

"Not at all." He held out his hand. "Matt Sorensen of The Darlington Law Group in Palm Beach. Pleased to meet you."

She shook his hand. "Please, have a seat in the living room."

"Mind if I join you?" McKay asked.

"That's up to Darcy." Matt glanced at her.

"I'd like Dad to be included, whatever this is about," she said. "Can I get you something to drink?"

"No thanks, let's get right to it." Matt set his briefcase on the coffee table and opened it. He pulled out a document while Darcy and her father sat on the couch.

He glanced from Joe to Darcy. "This is the Last Will and Testament for Mr. Earl Stanton, recently deceased."

She gasped. "What has the will of a serial killer got to do with me?"

"First, let me assure you my law firm had no knowledge of Stanton's criminal activities, nor did we know what was in his will. He brought it to us in a sealed envelope and had us witness his sworn statement on the outside of the envelope, attesting that it was his will and that it should not be opened until after his death."

"Okay, I believe you're not a bad person, but why would you bring his will here? I never even met the man," she said.

"Earl Stanton was very clever. He managed to fool everyone for years while he murdered young women right under the noses of wealthy people attending parties at his mansion. I believe you found seventeen bodies buried on his estate and his own body in his secret basement."

"That's true, she and her trained dogs found them," McKay said.

"Stanton decided if anyone ever managed to uncover his crimes, the buried bodies, et al, he would reward that person after his death by leaving him or her all his worldly possessions." Matt smiled at Darcy. "You found all the bodies and the note about the contents of Earl's safe, enabling the police to identify all the victims." He shrugged. "I read the police report."

"Wait, are you saying I'm supposed to inherit his estate?" she asked.

"Yes, it'll take time to transfer everything into your name, but you'll get his forty-acre estate and everything on it, all his companies, his investment portfolios, bank accounts, cars, yachts, corporate jet—it's a long list. My firm will help you with everything, including the estate taxes. Just sign here and here." He pointed at separate lines on the document. "This just verifies that I informed you of your inheritance."

"Holy cow! I'm not sure how I feel about this— inheriting from a serial killer." She shook her head.

The chief smiled. "Darcy, this means you can keep your Sniffers Agency and use the money to do a lot of good in this world." He elbowed her. "Sign the paper."

Matt handed her a pen and the document.

She took a deep breath, exhaled slowly, and signed it.

Matt said, "As soon as the police release the crime scene, you can take possession of the mansion and everything on the forty-acre estate. You'll also have access to the money in his bank accounts here in the States later this week. The foreign holdings will take longer to finalize. Your Gulfstream G650 jet is hangered at Millionaire Aviation at the Palm Beach International Airport, and your two-hundred-foot yacht is docked at the Palm Beach Yacht Club. The sixty-foot yacht is docked at his estate's pier on Diamond Lake. We'll sort everything out and get back to you later this week." He stood and closed his briefcase.

Darcy and her father walked Matt to his car and waved goodbye. As he drove away, Scott passed him on his drive in. His engine made its usual clanking noise as he shut it off.

She and her father waited while he exited the car.

"Your engine's not sounding too good," Chief McKay said.

"I'm afraid it's just about reached its expiration date, but I think it'll last long enough for me to take your lovely daughter out for a nice dinner." He smiled at Darcy. "Ready to go?"

She grinned. "I sure am. I'll just grab my purse."

She winked at her father and whispered, "Don't tell," as she hurried into the house.

McKay put his hand on Scott's shoulder. "Detective, this may turn out to be the best date you've ever had."

FORTY-NINE

A week later, Scott pulled into the ranch to pick up Darcy. His car still made the clanking noise. She met him on the driveway and kissed him.

"Ready to go?" He opened her door.

"I was born ready." She grinned and hopped in. "We'll have fun dancing with our friends tonight. I'm so happy Sandy is coming too. We just need to make one stop first."

"Okay, where to?"

"Banyan Country Estates. I promise it won't take long."

He reached over and squeezed her hand. "Anything for you, girlfriend."

Fifteen minutes later, she pulled an electric gate

opener from her purse. "Turn in here." She opened the tall, wrought-iron gates.

"Darcy, this is the Stanton estate. What are we doing here?"

"You'll see. Take the driveway up to the garage." She pointed.

When Scott parked in front of the huge garage, she pushed a button on her device that opened the garage doors. The light came on, revealing six super cars and an empty spot where the luxury SUV had been parked.

She explained, "Stanton left everything to me because my dogs and I found him out. Pick one. I hope you don't mind that I already gave the Range Rover Autobiography to my dad."

In moments, Scott was grinning from ear to ear as he drove away with Darcy in his black McLaren 720S Spider.

EPILOGUE

Darcy paid off the mortgage on her father's ranch and gave him ten million dollars. Law enforcement was in Joe's blood, so he chose to remain as Garnet's Chief of Police.

Two months later, Chief Joe McKay proposed to his girlfriend, Sally, and she said yes. By then, Darcy had moved into the former Stanton estate. The secret part of the basement that had been used to imprison and kill young women had been filled with concrete, and a special memorial garden for the victims had been planted on the property.

Ray Stanton was serving a life sentence in a prison for the criminally insane. Sandy Barker and Tina and David

Trent had fully recovered physically. For Sandy and Tina, their emotional recoveries would take longer.

Now that Darcy had complete ownership of Stanton's assets, she gave two million dollars to each family that had lost a daughter to Stanton, and she also gave two million each to Sandy Barker, Tina Trent, and David Trent. It was forty-two million dollars well spent. The money would never make up for their losses and traumas, but it helped make their lives easier.

Now that Sandy could afford to quit her job at Dye to be Beautiful hair and nail salon, she became a full-time mystery author. Her first book, *Murder in Banyan Country Estates*, based on a true story, became a national best-seller.

Darcy had big plans for helping wounded military veterans, homeless people, homeless animals, and many worthy charities. She also had big plans for her handsome boyfriend, Detective Scott Logan.

And Scott had big plans for Darcy.

The Sniffers Agency had a fancy new office on the estate, and all their cases were accepted pro bono. Max, Dobie, Laddie, Tiny, and Daisy had luxury doggie beds cushioned with temper foam, a special swimming pool and play fountain, and their own chef who prepared delicious and healthy meals for them.

Sylvester had an unlimited supply of his favorite crackers, a household staff, and a huge estate to run. He'd even learned how to sweet talk the horses.

Life was good in Banyan Country Estates.

THE END

About the Authors

Dorothy Metz Littlefield has been writing for over fifty years. Her first story, *When Time Stood Still*, was published in magazines and in short-story anthologies.

Dorothy is currently writing mystery and romance novels as well as short stories. She draws on experiences from her world travels with her daughter, aerobatic flying, soaring, diving, hang gliding, horseback riding, and hot-air ballooning with her children.

Born and raised in Chicago, Illinois, she moved to Diamond Lake, Michigan after marrying her husband, Ken. They raised their two children, Sharon and Larry, in Michigan and later in Bradenton, Florida.

Dorothy was a long-time resident of Kilgore, Texas, where she raised horses on her ranch until she moved to West Palm Beach, Florida in 2002 to be near her children.

A child at heart, Dorothy and her daughter Sharon co-wrote *Journey into the Land of the Wingless Giants,* a middle-grade children's adventure novel that includes accurate details about wildlife and numerous examples of good morals. They also co-wrote *Enchanted,* a novella for young children, and an adult short-story anthology, *Life, Love, & Laughter: 50 Short Stories.*

Sharon Littlefield Menear is a retired airline pilot. US Airways hired Sharon in 1980 as their first female pilot, bypassing the flight engineer position. The men in her new-hire class gave her the nickname Bombshell. She flew Boeing 727s and 737s, DC-9s, and BAC 1-11 jet airliners and was promoted to captain in her seventh year.

Before her pilot career, Sharon worked as a water-sports model and then traveled the world as a flight attendant with Pan American World Airways.

Sharon also enjoyed flying antique airplanes, experimental aircraft, and Third World fighter airplanes. Her leisure activities included scuba diving, powered paragliding, snow skiing, surfing, horseback riding, aerobatic flying, sailing, and driving sports cars and motorcycles.

Sharon has flown many of the airplanes in her action thriller novels, *Flight to Redemption*, first place winner of the Royal Palm Literary Award, *Flight to Destiny*, *Triple Threat*, *Stranded*, and *Vanished*, Books One - Five in the *Samantha Starr Series* featuring a woman airline pilot. A sixth book in the series will be released in 2022.

Sharon has a new mystery/suspense series, The Jettine Jorgensen Mysteries. *Dead Silent*, Book 1, will be released in August 2021. Darcy and her Sniffers Agency will return in *Dropped Dead*, Book 2 in the Jettine Jorgensen Mysteries in early 2022.

Sharon and her mother also wrote a short-stories anthology book, *Life, Love, & Laughter: 50 Short Stories by S.L. Menear and D.M. Littlefield*.

S.L. Menear's web site: https://www.slmenear.com
Author's Facebook page: www.Facebook.com/slmenear

All books by authors S.L. Menear and D.M. Littlefield are available in soft cover and eBooks at major online retail sites, and on request at bookstores.

A Request from the Authors

We hope you enjoyed our cozy mystery. May we ask a favor? Please post a review on the site where you purchased it or on goodreads.com. Your brief review might help someone else decide whether they'd like to read our book. We, like all authors, live and die by readers' reviews. Please help us out so we can continue to entertain you with future books. Thank you.

Warm regards,
Sharon and *Dottie*